Quit Breaking My Heart

Jenica Johnson

D1715549

0 0022 0502572 5

ALL RIGHTS RESERVED. No part of this publication may be reproduced, distributed or transmitted in any form or by any means, including photocopying, recording, or other electronic or mechanical methods, without the prior written permission of the publisher, except in the case of brief quotations embodied in critical reviews and certain other noncommercial uses permitted by copyright law. For more information, please contact the publisher.

Copyright © 2017 Jenica Johnson

Published by Jenica Johnson Presents

Note: This is a work of fiction. Names, characters, places and incidents either are products of the author's imagination or are used fictitiously. Any resemblance to actual events or locales or persons, living or dead, is entirely coincidental.

Author Notes

Thank you to all my old readers and welcome to my new readers. This book was another challenge for me. Some events in this book may touch you because I strove to make this relatable to women. We go through so much heartbreak from men, family and sometimes our kids. Sometimes men don't realize the pain we have to endure. But, wait, men go through heartbreak too, which you will see in here as well. I hear a lot of people say, "Just leave," but sometimes it's not that easy. Soul ties are hard to break as you will see. And walking away from a marriage surely isn't easy. The heart is a tricky organ, but we must learn how to use it wisely.

You will notice in my upcoming writings there will be no more "Christian" views. I will still write clean for my readers who like a good, drama-filled clean book. There won't be any preaching going on in my books. I will still drop nuggets along the way, though. I can't help that. I don't want to be placed in a box. I want to open my laptop and freely write what comes to me without having a stigma. Some topics I would love to write about, but the "church" would kill me and throw me in hell, lol.

Again, thank you to each and every one of you who downloaded, shared links, discussed in book clubs and everything else you awesome readers do. It's appreciated, trust me. If you like my books, leave a review and tell a friend.

Link up with me:

Instagram: jenicajwrites

Twitter: @authorjenicaj

Paris

S itting at the table full of bourgeois females made my stomach flip. I continued to sip on my glass of Riesling and watch as they flashed their wedding rings in my face. I was still unsure why I had put on my best outfit to come here. I set my glass down and flipped my inches over my shoulder, making sure to hit my neighbor in the face. It was the only way to get her to shut up about her ugly, snotty nosed kids.

"Paris, what is it you do again?"

"I sleep around with men for money," I said before swallowing my drink and getting up.

The gasps at the table were just what I needed. It was my ten-year class reunion and all these females were still the same. None of them liked me because more than likely, their boyfriend was checking for me ten years ago. Females were my worst enemy. Besides my girl Cori, who was approaching me with a smile on her face.

"Where are you going?"

"I'm leaving. You know I never liked any of these people. Then y'all had the gall to sit me at the table with all the old cheerleaders. You knew what you were doing." I pointed my finger in her face playfully.

"Girl, get that finger out of my face. When we planned this reunion, we wanted everyone to mingle, so we sat everyone by last name. You know I wanted you by me, but the rest of the coordinators said to do it this way. I got a seat next to me; just don't leave, Paris," Cori begged.

"I guess I'll stay. It better be worth my while. I could be home with a bag of popcorn and my Fire Stick."

"You need a life, Paris."

"Oh, I got a life."

I joined Cori at her table, and to my surprise, my old high school crush was sitting at the table. He still looked as fine as he did ten years ago. The server placed a new wine glass in front of me. Before I could realize it, I had downed it and was asking for another one. He always made me nervous with the way he stared at me. Tonight, was no different. He sat right across from me, nursing his glass of water.

His name was Novi. He was a god. His teeth sparkled from the dim lighting and his skin was flawless. He had his hair cut close to his scalp; I really wasn't sure what they called it. His beard had a few grey hairs in it, which made him look really mature. We were only twenty-eight, but we could easily pass for twenty-five. He winked at me and I almost spit out my drink.

Cori hit knees with me under the table. That had been our signal since we were younger. I reached in my purse for my phone. I needed something to distract me from his gaze. I scrolled through my phone until I decided to open my Kindle app and read a book on my phone. The DJ slowed the music down and Cori hopped up and ran out on the floor with her husband, leaving me at the table with Novi.

"Would you like to dance?" His voice boomed over the music.

"Nah, I'm not much of a dancer."

"Aah, come on. You don't have to do nothing but sway your hips. It can't be that hard," he suggested.

I couldn't say no and embarrass him because he was now standing over me with his hand out. I put my phone down and placed my hand in his. His hands were so soft. I mean, cotton soft, y'all. Novi always took care of himself when we were in school. He played football, basketball and baseball, but he never looked dirty like most of the players. He kept his hair cut, nails clean and clothes ironed.

The song was changed, but it was still slow, so Novi grabbed the small of my back and brought me in closer to him. He smelled so good. It was a hint of sweet and spicy. I had a very sensitive nose, but I could smell him all night. Out of my peripheral, I could see Cori giving me the thumbs up. Cori knew firsthand all the trouble I had with men. I really hated men, but I loved them at the same time. I always fell for the ones who broke my heart. I just wanted someone to love me.

"What have you been up to since we been out of school?" Novi whispered in my ear.

I didn't feel like this was the perfect place to talk because I was struggling to stay on beat with the music. Instead of being rude, I stopped dancing and took his hand so we could go outside and talk.

"Why you brought me out here?"

"I couldn't dance and talk. I decided we would just talk," I replied.

"My bad," he laughed.

"What did you ask me again?"

"I asked, what you been doing since we got out of school?"

"Avoiding men."

"What?" He laughed again.

"Men are trash. It's like all y'all want is one thing. It's like, you got a girl, but want something else on the side too. I don't get it. So, lately, I've just been chilling and traveling. What about you?" I looked over at him.

"Besides playing ball across seas, I've been running my non-profit organization. Life for me is pretty boring."

"Sounds interesting to me. Definitely better than mine."

"I wouldn't say that. I don't have anyone to share all my happiness with. My mom died about two years ago and I've been lonely ever since then. You have no idea what it's like to be in a foreign land with no one to share it with."

"I'm sorry about your mother. I had no idea. I remember her being at all your games, cheering you on. She fed the whole team before the game and always had those dope Christmas parties for us. You had one of the coolest mothers ever," I told him.

"Yea, she was the bomb. I really miss her. I brought her over to Brazil with me and she got sick, so I sent her back home, but she was already in stage four of her breast cancer. I didn't think I was going to make it, but here I am. I told myself that I can make it through anything now."

"I've always wanted to go to Brazil. I heard it was beautiful over there."

"It is, but very dangerous and plagued with diseases if you're not careful. You should come visit me."

"I can't do that," I shyly said.

"Why not? Obviously, you've been feeling me since we were in school. Cori told me graduation night, but I was dating someone else at that time."

"I'm going to kill her." I started walking off before Novi grabbed my arm.

"No, it's cool. I always thought you were cool too. I just always had a girl on my hip. I wouldn't dare approach you knowing I was dating someone else. I'm free now."

"I'll have to think about it."

"Well, let me know and I'll have everything set up for you. Where's your phone? I want to give you both of my numbers. I really enjoyed talking to you. I know there's a lot more to you, but I guess I'll peel your layers back the more I get to talk to you."

"Yea, I guess so. My phone is at the table. We can exchange numbers there."

We entered the building again and everyone was on the dance floor, which was good. I didn't need any attention on me. I hated people watching my every move. The table I was sitting at earlier was empty, but when my eyes went to the dance floor, they were all pointing at Novi and me. I shot all of them a bird and proceeded to give Novi my phone and he gave me his.

I said my goodbyes to Novi and snuck out before Cori could stop me. I was in desperate need of my bed. My anxiety was running high from hanging around all those people and I needed some peace. Cori was so charismatic and got along with everyone. I was usually the ghetto one, getting into fights and biting people's heads off.

Placing my key in the door, I could hear my Yorkie's collar ringing as she ran to the door. I bent down to pick her up as I threw my purse down and walked to my room. My laptop was still on my ex's Facebook page and I noticed I had a few messages. Yes, I was still obsessed with my ex. We were supposed to be married by now, but he ran off with some chick he met on the internet years ago. I spent most of my time trying to find ways to get him back, but my heart wouldn't let me.

I opened my messages to see my ex had hit me up saying he was in town. I put my dog down to respond. He had sent the message hours ago, but I would gladly go see him. He had it like that with me. I hit the send button on my response and waited patiently to see what he would say. After waiting a few more minutes, he never said anything back, so I removed my clothes and took my makeup off.

The dinging sound of Messenger on my phone woke me up out of my sleep. My ex responded and I knew there was only one thing he wanted if he was hitting me back at almost three in the morning. I agreed to meet him at his location. This was the reason I would never be a wife. Men had a way of having a wife or significant other, but would still reach out to get their needs met by another woman. I'd be a fool not to go because he always paid me well. My mortgage was in his name, and so was the nice Audi I drove. I got dressed comfortably and exited my house.

I pulled up to his old apartment he had moved into when he first started dating his new woman. Once he married her, he moved about forty-five minutes away and only came back when he wanted to have sex with me or question my whereabouts. I briskly walked up to the door and the door opened, but it was dark when I stepped in.

"Kenny, why is it so dark?" I nervously asked.

One yank of my neck signified what was going on. His wife had found out we were still messing around. She was pulling on my brand-new Cambodian hair I had spent my last on and I was about to give her the business. I dropped my purse and viciously swung back until I connected with something. The burning coming from my skin was slowing me down, though. My arm felt like it had been sliced open.

"Next time I hear about you, I'm going to kill you. I hate nasty females like you," she spat, before kicking me in my chest, knocking the wind out of me.

She snatched up my belongings and threw them out the door. She then grabbed me by my shirt and pulled me out the door.

"Leave Kenny and me alone. He will be deactivating his page and his number will be changed. Get off my doorstep." She slammed the door in my face.

I couldn't move right away because I was still trying to catch my breath. Thank goodness it was late and everyone was asleep. I put all my stuff back into my purse and got in my car. His wife was so dumb. Kenny would never leave me alone. We shared something deeper than she ever knew. That was why he paid me once a month faithfully: so I could keep my precious mouth closed. Her beating me up and cutting my arm was only going to add to my bank account when I talked to him. I headed to the hospital to get my arm checked out.

"Paris, I told you a long time ago to leave Kenny alone. Once he got married, he was no longer your man. He's only your baby daddy. It isn't like either of y'all are raising the baby. I'm raising him," Cori fussed.

"Don't throw that up in my face. You agreed as my friend to take on the responsibility. I make sure my son has everything he needs. Shoot, I even pay some of your bills."

"I'm not throwing it up in your face. I'm just reminding you that you have no reason to be seeing Kenny. This could've turned out a lot worse than it did. Now I'm here wrapping up your arm because you keep bleeding through the gauze," Cori fussed while wrapping the bandage tightly.

"Ouch!"

"I knew when you left the reunion in a hurry, it was because of some foolishness."

"No, it wasn't. Tell my son to come here so I can give him a kiss. I'm tired of you complaining already."

"There you go, trying to get rid of us, but we ain't going nowhere. Tell me about Novi. He left right after you did."

"What you want me to tell you? We talked and exchanged numbers, that's it."

"He's the kind you need to be with, instead of nasty Kenny."

"Whatever, Cori. I'm not like you. I can't find a man to marry me and give me the world."

"Oh, please. Let's be honest, Paris; you have a type."

"Is something wrong with that?"

"Yes, if your type belongs to someone else."

"Kenny was mine first. She came along and took him," I finished.

"That is somewhat true. Did you not steal Kenny from another woman? Oh, okay."

"I swear I can't win with you."

"No, I'm just not going to baby you," Cori stated.

I was so glad my phone had started ringing because Cori was starting to give me a headache. She snatched the phone before I could get to it.

"Look here, you dog, stop calling her unless it pertains to your child. You could've got her killed last night," Cori fussed.

"Give me my phone, Cori."

Kenny was yelling because I could clearly hear him. They hated each other. Cori was raising our child because she loved me, although I was stable enough to raise a child. I really hated kids, but I had slipped up and forgotten to take my birth control, and here I was, someone's mother. I rarely spent time with my child. If I did, it was because Cori made me.

I got out of bed to grab the phone from her ear. Kenny was still fussing and calling her out of her name. Cori gave me a scowl before she snatched her stuff up and stormed out the room.

"Kenny, it's me. You can stop all that yelling," I told him.

"Why is she answering your phone?"

"She got to it before I could. I mean, your wife did cut my arm last night."

"I'm sorry about that. I had no idea she even drove over there. She told me she was going to the grocery store."

"How the hell you didn't know she was missing for that long?" I quizzed.

"Look, we don't be down each other's throat like that. She does her and I do me," he explained.

"Some kind of marriage arrangement you guys have," I huffed.

"I didn't call to argue. I'm about to deposit some funds into your account to cover your medical bills and maybe go shopping for you and Kj."

Kenny thought money made me feel better when it was love I was looking for. I gave Kenny the best years of my younger life. I had men tell me that Kenny would never marry me, but I stuck it out, thinking they were just jealous. The first female who showed him a little interest, he left me high and dry. I was eight months pregnant when he walked out on me and he paid me to keep my mouth closed about our son.

"Kenny—"

"Look out the window," he interrupted.

In the space that Cori had just been occupying was a brand new 2017 Lincoln Continental. A smile so big spread across my face. I forgot all about my arm as I rushed to put a jacket on so I could run outside to see all the features it had.

"Do you like it?"

"I love it."

"Good. I'll be there in a few days. I'm about to give you my other number that she has no idea about."

"Okay," I replied before hanging up.

Kenny was a rich boy from Texas. His parents struck rich with an oil rig. They moved to Georgia when he was about thirteen. Kenny's father hated me, but I hated him more. He looked down on me like I was a poor sister from the hood. Kenny and I met our ninth grade year in algebra class. He was having a hard time comprehending the math, so I slid my pretty self right in his lap when he posted a flyer for a tutor. I held an A in the class, so why wouldn't I help him? Who said a girl from the hood wasn't smart?

I played around with all the new gadgets in the car. The smell of a brand-new car was intoxicating, and this was one of my weaknesses. The last thing I needed was a new car but I would be a fool to reject it. I wasn't supposed to be driving since I had taken a pain pill for my arm, but I was desperate to see how the car drove.

After taking the car around the corner, I ended up back in the house, in the bed. As exciting as it was to have a new car, the loneliness always set in when I was home alone. I was thinking about taking Novi up on his offer to go to Brazil. What did I have to lose? I wasn't committed to anyone at the time. Before I drifted off to sleep, I texted Novi to tell him I would love to come to Brazil to visit him. Once he responded, I was able to sleep peacefully.

Cori

"Come on, Kj, so you can get in the bed!" I yelled down the hall.

My life wasn't as easy as my best friend Paris thought. She passed her son off to me like I wasn't battling with staying pregnant with my own children. I loved Kj just like he was mine, but my husband wanted his own children. I knew it wouldn't be long before he stepped out on me. He treated me like royalty, but in the back of my mind, I figured there was another woman.

"I'm coming, Auntie Cori. Uncle Mari was beating me in 2K."

Kj was turning seven soon and he still didn't know who his father was; he barely knew Paris. Anytime I dropped him off, he begged for me to stay with him. He said all Paris did was complain about him messing her house up. I hated when I picked him up and he came out sad.

"Maybe you can beat him tomorrow, but you have school tomorrow."

"Auntie Cori, why were you mad at Mommy Paris?"

"That's not for you to worry about. All I need your little brain to worry about is school. I love you." I kissed his forehead.

I closed the door slightly before I slipped into Mari's man cave to spend some time with him. He worked seven days a week most weeks, so time was limited with us two. He was engulfed in his game but looked up to give me a smile and a nod to sit next to him. He gave me the other controller and we went a few rounds in the game. That was our way of relieving the stress of the day before we even spoke words. No one understood our relationship, but we did. That was why we were so successful with our marriage, except having kids.

"How was your day, bae?" he asked as he turned the game off.

"It was hectic, but let me hear about yours first."

"Same old thing with me. Dudes calling in, dudes complaining about working overtime and a supervisor who gets on my nerves," Mari stated.

"Well, I appreciate you dearly. Kj and I can't do anything without you."

"Thanks, baby. You know I'll do anything for y'all. Now, tell me about your girl."

"Mari, I don't know what I'm going to do with her. She just doesn't get it. I went over there to help her get from the hospital

19

and make sure she had something to eat and to let her see her son. Kenny calls and she just about breaks her neck to get to the phone."

"She's looking for love in the wrong places," Mari stated.

"Well, Kenny is definitely the wrong place. He went off and married another woman and then, this same woman lures Paris to Kenny's old place, just to jump on her. She needs to check her man and not Paris. I know she would die if she knew they had a child together. Oh, and as Kj and I were pulling off, he had a car dropped off for her. The nerve of him."

"One thing I always tell you, remain loyal. Don't let her use you, but just be her friend. Paris is a lost soul. It's all in her eyes."

Mari was big on friendship. He rarely talked to Paris because he disliked the fact she gave her child up for a man who wasn't worried about her. He made sure our friendship stayed consistent for Kj's sake. I loved Mari because of his wisdom. He was a product of his environment. Raised by his grandmother, he did jail time and worked hard to prove he had a spot in society. He was almost done with his degree and I knew things would change once he finished.

"I'm about to head to bed. I got a double tomorrow and then I got to go to the school to take a test too."

"I'll be in there in a minute. You know I got to clean this house up before I come to bed."

"Ain't nothing wrong with this house. You OCD." He laughed before kissing my lips.

I didn't work, so I felt it was my responsibility to make sure he had a meal and clean house. I didn't work because Mari didn't want me to. He claimed he watched his grandmother work two and three jobs to take care of him and his other cousins. I hated not bringing anything to the table. Mari made sure we had everything and more, but I couldn't give him the one thing he desired. I blamed it on him being stressed, but I would never tell him that. That was the reason I had made a doctor's appointment, just to make sure it wasn't me.

♥

I dropped Kj off to school and made sure Mari was gone to work before I got dressed for my appointment. I was now in an empty room with all this equipment, naked from the waist down, waiting for the doctor to come in and check my uterus. This was something I would usually bring Paris to, but she wasn't responding to any of my text messages last night or this morning. I played on my phone until the door opened and a small, foreign doctor stepped in.

"Mrs. Carter, I'm Doctor Sam."

"Nice to meet you."

"So, I hear you're having problems conceiving?"

"Well, I've conceived three times, but I miscarried all of them. That was about three years ago. I just find it strange I haven't gotten pregnant in three years. My husband doesn't use any protection."

"I see. We can find out if there is anything going on with your womb and if so, we can talk about your options. I'll be using this sonogram machine, but I will insert this doppler into your vagina. I'll be taking pictures of your uterus and your fallopian tubes. You'll feel pressure, but nothing more. Before we start, I always like to have a female nurse in here with me. Oh, and there she goes."

The nurse flipped the lights off and assisted Doctor Sam with wrapping the doppler with a big plastic condom looking thing. She put the lube on and he talked to me through the whole thing. I watched as he maneuvered inside of me. All he would do was mumble, which made me nervous. The nurse would give me a comforting smile, but I wanted to know what the issue was that had him mumbling to himself. He snapped some pictures and wrote notes. The procedure was over in fifteen minutes.

"Mrs. Carter," he said, taking his gloves off.

The nurse helped me sit up and I waited for him to wash his hands.

"Is something wrong?" I questioned.

"Your uterus sits back pretty far, but that won't stop you from carrying a baby. I did see a lot of scar tissue in there from your previous miscarriages. I still can't say that's the problem. You seem to be healthy. I would love to see your husband so we can get to the bottom of this. Do you think he would come in? Most husbands don't like the idea of others being in their business, and I get it. I'm a doctor who wants to see women carry healthy babies. I want to help, so if you can get him to see me, we can move forward," he finished.

"Thank you, Doctor Sam."

I cleaned myself up before I put my clothes back on. I didn't make my next appointment because I needed to talk to Mari. I could talk to him about anything, but this whole baby situation was a very sensitive subject in my marriage. After we had lost our second child, he was done. He didn't eat for weeks and lost close to seventy-five pounds afterward. We still had sex, but he was always worried. He always said he didn't want to take my body through it again, but I believed it was him who didn't want to go through the devastation again.

I decided to swing by Paris' before I went home to start my everyday routine of cooking and cleaning. Both of her cars were in the driveway, so I knew she was home. I hit the doorbell and beat on the door. She hadn't gotten her mail this morning, so she was probably still asleep. Paris never slept long because she was usually somewhere spending Kenny's money. The way her mink hair looked yesterday, I thought for sure she would be at the salon.

"Paris, it's Cori. I was coming by to check on you. Call me back when you get this message." I ended the call.

I prepped my food for tonight. Mari had called and told me he wouldn't be home until close to ten. To me, that was perfect because Kj would be in bed and I could talk to him as he ate his dinner and while he was a little tired. I fed Kj, ran his bath, helped him with his homework, and now he was in bed. I cleaned the kitchen and waited on Mari.

The door swung open with a tired Mari coming through it. I rose to get his food warmed up and help him out of his sweaty work clothes.

"Do you want to eat or shower first?"

"Let me shower, then I'll eat."

I stopped the food in the microwave to run his water. This was my life, but I wanted to be in the workforce. I was scared to even tell Mari I wanted to get a job. I felt like a personal maid to him and Kj. I had a degree in marketing that I couldn't even use. My parents still fussed about paying for me to go to college for nothing. I felt like a failure. I put a smile on my face as my husband stepped out the shower, drying off and then throwing on some clothes to come and eat.

"Thank you, baby," Mari said with a mouth full of food.

"You're welcome. How did you do on your test?"

"Passed it with flying colors. I got two more, then it's graduation time."

"I went to the doctor today," I blurted out.

"You okay?" He raised his bushy eyebrow.

Mari was so handsome. He was light-skinned with hazel eyes and one dimple on his right cheek. He wore his hair cut a little on the wild side, only keeping the sides faded. He rarely dressed up because he was always working, but when he did dress up, he was the sexiest man on earth to me.

"Yes, I'm fine. I went to see why I hadn't gotten pregnant."

"Cori, I thought we talked about this. Don't bring this back up. When it's meant for us to have a baby, we will have one. There was no need for you to go running to the doctor."

"I just wanted to make sure I wasn't the problem."

"You're not the problem, baby. I cannot have this conversation with you tonight. I'm too tired."

"Will you see if you're the problem?"

"What!" Mari laughed.

"I'm twenty-six years old. I'm younger than you. Why would I have a problem? I'm young and healthy, baby. Don't try me like that."

"I'm not saying it like that. You're only two years younger than me. Don't make it seem like you're a spring chicken. Most people our age have two and three kids by now. I was just thinking, maybe the stress was stopping you from performing."

"Performing? I perform very well and you know that. Must I pull footage? Maybe I do work too much, but that has nothing to do with us conceiving. When it's our time, it's our time. We'll have so many babies, you're going to complain and beg me to stop."

"It was just a thought," I murmured.

Mari got up to give me a kiss before he left me in the kitchen, sitting at the table. I didn't move for at least an hour. I sat there, holding back my frustration and tears. Mari has been this way since we've been together. I never got to explain myself without him shutting me out. I left his plate on the table and grabbed a blanket from the closet so I could sleep on the sofa tonight. My love was shown every day in this house and I never asked for anything. The one thing I asked for, it was rejected. I was about to show Mari how it felt not to compromise.

"So, this is what we're doing now?" Mari stood over me.

I rubbed the sleep out of my eyes and turned the television on to see what time it was.

"Why didn't you come to bed?" Mari questioned.

"No reason."

"Don't be childish because I don't want to do what you want me to do, Cori. You know what, I'll see you when I get off."

I wasn't trying to start anything in my marriage, but last night, I noticed my husband wasn't going to ever agree on anything I wanted to do. I got Kj off to school and started my process of finding a job. There was no need in wasting away if I wasn't going to be a mother. I read an article in the paper about a magazine company hiring a marketing specialist, so I made sure I was dressed appropriately before I entered the business.

"Mrs. Carter," a blonde woman called my name out.

I stood up, straightening my skirt out before I walked up to her and shook her hand. I had only come in to fill out the application, but the receptionist told me to give her a minute and here I was, about to have my first interview. The sweat was starting to seep through my pores once she shut the door and there sat two other gentlemen.

"You can have a seat. Don't be nervous, this is just how we conduct our interviews. We work as a team around here. I'm Martha, this is Syeer, and Abe on the end. The receptionist gave us your application. Now, I see you have no job experience, but you do hold a degree in marketing. Why is it you've never worked?"

"Well, I got married at an early age and my husband never wanted me to work. I then took on my best friend's child and I'm raising him. I just feel like it's time for me to do something for myself for once."

"Well, in this area, we don't have a lot of people with marketing degrees. I'm interested in bringing you on. We will be training you and your salary will be very competitive. Do you think this is something you'll be interested in? You can start first thing Monday morning."

"Yes…yes!"

"Okay, so, I'll email you everything you'll need in the next few days and we'll see you Monday at 9 a.m."

"Thank you guys so much." I stood up to shake everyone's hands.

There was something behind Syeer's handshake. It was like electricity. I snatched my hand away and shook Abe's hand before leaving out. A smile so big spread across my face. I finally felt like I had accomplished something. I thanked the receptionist for her help as I went on about my day. I still hadn't heard from Paris, and I was becoming concerned. I got in the car and called her to give her the good news.

"Hello?" Paris said.

"Hey, girl, I have some great news."

"Make it quick, I'm trying to catch a flight."

"A flight? Where are you going?" I asked.

"I'm going to Brazil for a little while. I need a change of scenery," Paris confessed.

"With Novi? Paris, please be careful. What are you going to do about Kj?"

"He'll be fine. Just tell him I'm on vacation."

"Ugh, this is crazy. Just be careful and call me when you land."

I didn't even have time to tell her my good news. Paris stressed me out like she was my child. I ended up at the mall to do some shopping for my new job. I didn't do much because as much as Paris thought we were rich, we weren't. Mari made sure we lived comfortably and we had a cushion to fall back on, but it was nothing like Paris thought. I took my few sale items to the register and waited for her to ring them up. The most annoying voice interrupted the cashier and me.

"I swear I hate shopping with you. Why can't you just get your wife to do this type of stuff for you? I'm just here for one thing."

"Please shut up. That's why I don't come in public with you. My wife can't dress me because she can barely dress herself. She's so old fashion."

I turned back around to give the cashier my debit card for my purchase, she bagged my stuff, and I walked out of the store. When I got in the car, I finally let my tears fall. I didn't know my husband felt that way about me. I looked down at my old clothes and thought it was cute. Was he cheating on me with her? I wasn't the confrontational type. I let Paris do all that for me. After crying about ten minutes, I sucked it up and headed home. Kj had begged to ride the bus home with his friends, so that gave me time to get myself together before he got there. I thrived on him being in a stable home. I didn't want him to see me down because his uncle was a weak man and couldn't face me like a man.

Just for the heck of it, I called his phone to see if he would answer. To my surprise, he did.

"Hey, baby, is something wrong?"

"Umm, I was wondering what time you were coming home."

"I'm actually on the way home now."

"Oh, okay. I guess I'll see you when you get here."

I hung up the phone and went to hang up the clothes in the closet. I didn't want him to know I had been in the same store as him. Since Mari was keeping secrets, I wasn't going to tell him about my job. I was still unsure of how I was going to act towards him when he got here. I could still hear the woman's voice in my head. She was short and bright skinned. She wore her hair in blonde and brunette braids. Her style was definitely different from mine.

I walked into my bathroom and looked at my appearance. I wasn't ugly. I wore my hair in its natural state. It wasn't long, but I was far from baldheaded. I had worn glasses since I was ten years old. I looked into Lasik surgery but couldn't afford it. I was short, standing at only five feet even. I wasn't bright like Mari's female friend. I was brown with a blemish here or there. My weight was average for my height. Mari always picked and said I was skinny, but I was content with my weight.

The sound of Kj's feet padding against the floor broke me out of my trance.

"Auntie Cori, I passed my test today."

"I'm so proud of you. I've got to reward you, as usual," I laughed.

"Can I call my mama and tell her?"

"I think your mama is out of town, but we can try later."

"Well, can I go next door to my friend's house until you finish cooking?"

"Yes, and be careful, Kj."

"I will."

He threw his book bag down in the middle of the floor and ran back out the door, bumping into Mari on the way out.

"Watch where you going, boy!" he yelled at him.

He had an obvious attitude from the tone in his voice. I loved my husband, but I loved Kj more. I didn't know if his female friend had pissed him off on the way home, but I needed him to get it in check before he walked through the door. He walked up to me and pecked my lips and I could smell the cheap Bath & Body Works on him.

"What you cooking?" Mari asked.

"Hot dogs and slaw," I expressed.

"I don't want no hot dog, Cori."

"Well, I don't know what to tell you. I cook a hot meal every night. I think dogs will be good for us tonight," I said sarcastically.

"You know where I'll be at."

I waved my hand at his back and turned the pot on for the hot dogs. He was going to eat these hot dogs, with his doggish self.

Good for him. I couldn't wait until Monday morning.

Paris

"Thank you for flying International Brazil," the flight attendant spoke in broken English.

I pulled the cover to my window up to look at the scenery and it was gorgeous. Blue water, green mountains and colorful plants. This was by far the longest flight I'd been on and I was exhausted. We were finally able to take our seat belts off and exit the plane. Novi was nice enough to get a first-class ticket, which I knew was a pretty penny, but it wasn't my money, so I didn't care. I grabbed my purse and carry-on bag so I could make my exit. Novi had texted me and told me a driver would be waiting and to look for my name.

I walked around for about thirty minutes looking for my name. I couldn't understand anything the people here were saying, so there was no need for me to stop and ask for directions. I was finally able to make it to the front of the airport. My feet were aching from wearing these heels, but I refused to be mediocre in Brazil, so I was being a little extra with my high heels and cat suit.

"Aaahh, thank God," I yelped as I saw the man holding my name up.

"Miss Pari," he spoke in broken English.

"It's Paris. With an S."

"Yes, Paris."

"Whatever." I waved him off.

He grabbed my luggage and placed it in the car. The climate here was dry and humid. I was glad I had spent a little extra getting my hair redone because it would've looked like a bird's nest if I hadn't. I texted Novi to let him know I was in the car and headed to him. I was so excited to see him. It felt good to be in a different country for a change, not thinking about Kenny and his cheating ways. And, as much as I loved Cori, I just couldn't get over the fact that she was so naïve and thought her husband wasn't cheating on her. I mean, I'd tried to tell her, but she never listened. I guess once I made it back from this little vacation, I was just going to come out and say it. If we were no longer friends, then so be it, but I couldn't have it on my chest any longer.

The car came to a stop and I looked up long enough to see where I would be staying. Now, I wasn't the smartest crayon in the box, but I knew over here, they didn't pay basketball players very well. This house was enormous. I stepped out when Novi emerged from the house, looking like a piece of dark chocolate on Easter Sunday. His smile was like ten thousand stars shining as he walked towards me.

"God, keep me near the cross," I whispered as he flexed his chest at me.

"I'm so glad you made it. How was your flight?" Novi asked.

"It was long, but worth it." I smiled.

"Well, let's get you comfortable, so the fun can begin."

"Novi, I had no idea you were living like this," I gleamed.

"I don't mention it very often. It either draws the wrong woman or makes the right one run away.

"I'll have you in your own room while you're here unless you want to join me. Either way, I just want you to be comfortable while you're here. Hopefully, you'll like it here and you won't leave." He winked.

Novi left me in my room. It was the size of my place back home. I dove on the massive bed, kicking my shoes off. The comforter was so cozy. I closed my eyes and opened them to see mirrors on the ceiling. I saw them in movies, but never in real life. I laid there just admiring my body from below. Kj had left some good weight on me and I was thankful. I got off the bed to explore the room a little more. The closet was full of his clothes and shoes, so I checked out the bathroom. It was a woman's dream. It was draped in gold and ivory.

I was going to pry over dinner. I couldn't be here in Brazil, getting locked up because Novi was doing something illegal. Cori would kill me.

There was a note on the sink that read: *Be ready by 8.*

I looked at my watch to see what time it was. I still had time to get some sleep. My body was tired from the flight and time change. I slipped out of my cat suit and got under the cover. The curtains were open, so it took a little longer than expected to go to sleep. When my brain relaxed, so did my body and I was off to La-la Land.

"Wake up, sleepy head." Novi shook me.

I covered my face with the cover. I didn't want him to see all the slobber on my arm and my hair sticking up.

"I'm up," I said from under the cover.

"I only came because it was past 8 and you never showed up. If you're tired, we can hang out tomorrow. I'll have some food sent to you."

"Can we stay in tonight, please?" I asked.

"Sure. Don't stay cooped up in the room. Once you rest up, come find me."

I shot from under the cover when he walked out. I was a horrible sleeper. Kenny was the only man who was able to see me when I woke up without my face on. I wasn't ugly, but I had a few insecurities. I managed to get up and fix myself up before

I came out the room. The house was so big, I had no idea where I was going. All I knew was my stomach was talking to me and I needed to find something to eat, fast. I made it downstairs where the aroma of food was coming from. I wasn't a big fan of trying new foods, but since I was going to spend so much time here, there was a chance something new was going to touch my taste buds.

"There she is. I was just getting your food ready to come up to your room. Now that you're here, you might as well join me," Novi said.

He was so good looking. His chiseled chest and arms were like pieces of dark wood carved to perfection. His eyes were so deep, it was like looking into a never-ending galaxy. I was hypnotized and I couldn't move.

"Umm, Paris," Novi interrupted.

"Oh, I'm sorry. Sure, yea, I'll join you."

We were served rice with some type of red gravy. It smelled spicy and spices always tore my stomach up. I assumed the meat was chicken, but I was unsure. From the look on my face, Novi knew I was questioning what was sitting in front of me.

"It's chicken, just cooked a different way. The rice is like a Spanish rice and the red sauce is a special blend they cover everything with that is very delicious," Novi explained.

37

"Are you sure?"

"Why would I lie to you?" He smiled.

"I'm sorry. I'm just not a fan of new foods."

"Well, we're going to change that. Try it, and I bet you'll like it."

I dipped my fork into the rice, picking up just enough to get a taste. I put the food into my mouth and Novi was right, it was good.

"See, I told you."

We had enjoyed dinner and dessert before we went out on his balcony that overlooked the city. Our conversation flowed easily because he kept the focus on me. I had a few questions to ask him, as soon as he took a breath from asking me everything.

"Do you have kids?" Novi asked.

I choked on my glass of wine I had been sipping on. What kind of personal questions was he asking?

"No," I lied.

"I thought for sure someone would've wifed you up by now. You were always so pretty to me. Most of the girls like you have kids, a dog, nice house, and the perfect husband."

"I'm not that girl." I gulped the rest of my drink down.

He was getting really personal. What more could he ask about my life? I poured myself another glass of expensive wine. I needed to be drunk to deal with him.

"What about STDs and sexual partners? How many partners have you had? When was your last visit to the doctor?"

"What!"

"These are things I have to ask. I hope you don't think I brought you over here to spend empty time with you. I have to make sure I'm protected," Novi explained and snapped his fingers.

His servant came with a tray. Novi pulled a stapled packet, along with a pen from the tray. He flipped to the last page and gave it to me.

"What is this?" I asked.

"That is a contract."

"For?" I flipped back to the front page.

"I've searched everywhere for a woman to satisfy my lifestyle. I'll be blunt. I need you to be my contract wife. All I ask is that you show up at all my games, please me whenever I ask, and bore at least one of my children, preferably a boy."

I sat and listened to Novi spill out all his requests. I went deaf after he said have his child. How many women had he done this to?

"Since I know you, I'll give you until the morning to make your decision. I'm about to head out on the town. If you need anything, buzz one of my staff."

I was left out on the balcony by myself to think. I could hear Novi revving the engine to his car before he pulled off into the night. My brain was hurting and I needed to hear a familiar voice, so I called Cori.

"Hey, I was worried about you. How is Brazil so far?" Cori asked.

She was always happy. No matter how terrible I treated her, she always showed love towards me.

"Brazil is gorgeous. I love it here already. How is Kj?"

"He's sleeping. You know we are in different time zones."

"That's right. I'm sorry."

"It's okay. I'm glad you asked about him. I couldn't sleep until I knew you were okay," Cori stated.

"I'm fine, now you can rest. Thank you, Cori. I know I don't say it enough, but I really do thank you."

"No problem. I love you, girly."

"I love you too. Goodnight."

I hung up and plugged my phone up to the charger. Cori was always the one to keep me calm. Growing up, I always wanted to switch lives with Cori. She meant a lot to me, I just had a hard time showing it because of my selfishness. I really couldn't help the way I acted. I was taught to behave the way I did.

My father was the most selfish man on earth. He married my mother because she was pregnant with me. He worked and came home when he wanted to. He never paid a bill and many nights, my mother starved to make sure I had something to eat. A few years passed and my mother started having different men, who I thought were my uncles, pop up. Our lives changed for the better. She was able to provide for us without the help of my father. My father left one night and never came back, but by then, my mother had opened a bank account and was sporting the latest fashion. By the time I was eleven, my father had a total of twelve kids. My mother would never tell me who they were, or even let me try to find out. I longed for a sibling relationship, so when I met Cori, we just clicked and the rest was history.

Sleep wouldn't come to me. I assumed it was because I was in a new place and didn't have a television to watch, so I tossed and turned. I rolled over to see a remote, but where was the television? I grabbed it and hit the power button, and appearing from the ceiling was a big screen projector. The brightness of the screen lit up the room. Every other channel was something in Portuguese.

Frustrated, I turned it off and got on my phone. Social media would have to put me to sleep tonight. I hit my Snapchat to see what was going on back home, but everyone had partied hours ago. I then went to Instagram to see what was popping. I didn't know what made me do it, but I hashtagged Novi's name. A bunch of pictures popped up, but the most recent one was from a beautiful, exotic woman. I knew it was recent because Novi had left here dressed in the same shirt with a few buttons undone. He was leaned back with his hand touching her breasts and she was cheesing like it was the best night of her life. I scrolled down to see that Novi loved the night life. I mean, I loved it, too, but I wasn't wilding in the club every time the doors were open. I had seen enough. I shut my phone off and forced myself to sleep.

The next day rolled around and the maid was in my room, opening the curtains and getting fresh towels for me. I wasn't an early bird, and I didn't like my sleep to be interrupted. I wasn't at home, so I stretched and got out of bed. The maid didn't speak English, so she nodded her head at me and walked out. I showered, flat ironed my hair and applied a little bit of makeup and gloss before I went down for breakfast.

Novi was watching a sports channel in Portuguese while he stuffed his mouth with eggs and bacon. He was so into the footage that he didn't know I was in the kitchen until I sat down next to him. He smiled at me and went back to watching the television. A plate was set in front of me and I was finally able to tell what I was eating.

"I'm glad you decided to be my wife. I'll be going ring shopping for you today, and we will go out on the town and enjoy each other's company. Paparazzi will be out, so remember to always smile. It comes with the territory. Women will be an issue, too, but you don't have to worry about me doing anything out of the normal," he went on.

"I see women flock to you, per Instagram."

"Oh, that's nothing. Maybe once they see how fine you are, they'll finally leave me alone."

"So, when is the wedding?"

"Next weekend. I'll allow you to fly back home and tie up anything there because my season is about to start in the next few weeks. I'll be gone to training and stuff like that, but I'll have plenty for you to do and money to spend. That always makes a girl happy, right?"

"Of course." I smiled as I sipped my orange juice.

I lived for money. I couldn't wait to be dripping in diamonds and drive the latest cars just to post to my page to tick Kenny off. All I needed was for him to catch wind of me being with another man and he was going to crawl back to me like a baby.

"Here's a black card. Go out and do some shopping. My drivers know where all the hot spots are. Enjoy yourself, and I'll see you back here tonight. Buy something nice and sexy to wear too."

I slid the black card in my bra and smiled like the Grinch when Novi excused himself from the table. Who knew coming here would have me being a wife with unlimited money. I could really get used to this. Now, I just had to make sure I poured all my birth control pills down the drain. I needed to get pregnant as soon as possible to solidify my spot.

I had done enough shopping to last me a year and was glad I didn't have to lift a finger. All my bags were brought to my room. Day was switching to night and I desired to take a bath and get my hair and makeup done. I pulled out a red bodycon dress with diamond encrusted gladiator heels. My whole outfit costs a little over eight thousand dollars. I had never spent that much money, but everything was so expensive here. I quickly showered and put my makeup on. My hair wasn't going to be a problem. The mink hair was bone straight and stopped right on the top of my behind. I ran the flat iron over my edges and then laid my baby hairs. I turned around to look at myself before I headed down to Novi.

"You look so beautiful." He kissed my cheek.

"Thank you."

"I see you didn't have any problems shopping today."

"No, I didn't."

"Let's go."

Novi opened the door for me as I climbed into his Maserati. We pulled up to a club and the line was around the corner. Just like he said, paparazzi was out and snapping pictures of us. He hadn't given me my ring yet, but I wasn't worried.

"Novi, is this your secret wife?" a man asked with his face covered.

"Please give us some space." Novi softly pushed him away.

We didn't even wait in the line. We made it inside the club and the women flocked to Novi, pushing me out the way. Novi grabbed my hand and pushed me through the ladies.

"Excuse me, ladies, I'm here with my wife."

"Where her ring at?" a manly looking chick asked.

I turned my nose up at her. I couldn't get locked up in another country for putting my foot up her behind. I just smiled as Novi walked us to a section to sit down. The same woman who was in his pictures was already there waiting, but when she saw me, her face changed. Who was this woman? She wasn't happy to see me, and she let Novi know by throwing her drink in his face before she walked off. Novi released my hand and yanked her by her hair. He did it in such a smooth way that no one saw him. I stepped closer to hear what he was about to tell her.

"Did you really waste your cheap drink on my expensive suit? You almost got my girl's dress messed up. If you got beef, don't take it out on me. I told you last night it was nothing personal between us. You just wanted pictures for your friends. I touched your boob and now you here, waiting for me like we a couple. Now, I need you to leave before I have you escorted out."

She took off running, busting her tail on the way out.

Cori

Today was my first day at work. Kj was good for the day and Mari was being his usual self, besides the fact that he was being extra sensitive to me. For the past three days, I was only doing the bare minimum to show him how it felt to be underappreciated. He caught on to it by day two and was constantly asking if I was feeling well or if there was anything he could do for me. I sent him off to work, and now, I was gearing up to head into the office.

I ran my hands over my outfit to knock the wrinkles out. I wore a pair of black flats because I wasn't that good with heels and I had my hair pulled back into a ponytail. I finished the look with my glasses. Satisfied, I got my purse and was out the door. Trying to beat traffic was crazy, but I made it thirty minutes early. When I arrived, they had my badge ready so I could enter the building and all other parts as well. I was greeted by Syeer as soon as I got off the elevator. He gave me a cup of coffee and smiled.

"I'll be showing you to your office and teaching you how to effectively do your job. I hope you catch on quick because this is a fast-paced job and we have major companies that depend on us to make it happen for them."

I swiftly walked behind him because his long legs took bigger strides than my short legs. He was talking and I was trying to take it all in until we reached my office, which was right next to his. I had a decent view of the pier and my office had a sofa and a personal bathroom. This was nice, not to mention the salary they were paying for a beginner.

"Here, let me power on your computer. These new Macs can be a bit confusing." He reached over me and I got a whiff of his cologne.

Girl, if you don't get yourself together, you better.

I scooted back to give him a little room to work. The screen powered on and he slid a chair next to me. I started perspiring under my arms. They were tingling so bad, I couldn't help maneuvering in my seat.

"You okay?"

"Yea. Yea, I'm fine."

"Okay, so this is your email. This is where we communicate almost all day. The only time our phones ring is if it's a client. Your workload is usually uploaded to the task master, which is here. Only thing you have on here is to fill out all your paperwork. You work on marketing, so once we get a product done, it's your job, well, our job to make sure we come up with something that will grab the customer's attention. What are some of the things customers like to see?"

"Colors, music, reviews and stuff like that," I nervously said.

"Okay…okay, you a'ight." He nudged me.

"Thank you." I pushed my glasses up on my face.

"I guess I'll leave you alone. All the forms you have to fill out are under here. It's for insurance and all that other stuff jobs need. If you need me, you can buzz me or walk over to my office."

"Thank you for everything." I smiled at him.

"That's what I'm here for. I'm about to get to work." He backed up into the door.

He was embarrassed, but I thought it was cute. He closed the door behind him as I was left to my thoughts and all this paperwork. The first form I pulled up was insurance. I started filling it out until I got to the married part. Mari didn't have insurance on me because he couldn't afford it at his job, so we had gotten a cheap policy on the outside that wasn't worth much but burial. Kj and I had Obamacare, but it was going to feel good to have regular insurance.

My phone buzzed in my purse. I didn't know the policy on taking phone calls, so I didn't answer. Instead of finishing the insurance forms, I went to the handbook so I could familiarize myself with the rules. I didn't want to get fired on my first day. My phone buzzed again, but this time, I answered it.

49

"Hello?" I said above a whisper.

"Where you at?" Mari questioned.

"I'm out, why?"

"I came home because I forgot something and you weren't there."

"What, am I supposed to sit home all day?"

"I mean, what else you gon' do, baby? You ain't got no job, so what you gon' do all day?"

"I got to go. I'll see you tonight."

"Wait, I'm working a double, so I won't see you until real late. Maybe like two or three in the morning. But then, I got to go right back at seven."

"A'ight, Mari."

"I love you."

"I love you too," I mumbled.

I fought the urge to cry. Hearing Mari tell me he loved me meant a lot; I just knew he didn't mean it. No man could truly love his wife and still find time for another woman. One of us was going to lack something. Mari worked hard, but never as much as he had been doing lately. I read through a few policies and greeted some co-workers as they walked by my office. They made me feel right at home here. I played around with my computer so I could become familiar with what they used.

"Hey, it's lunch time around here. Let's go grab something. There's a cafeteria downstairs that has pretty decent food if you don't want to leave," Syeer stated.

I looked at the time in the corner of my computer. I was so busy learning everything that I didn't notice how much time had passed.

"Okay, I am a little hungry."

"You can leave your purse. It's on me. You can lock your office, too, and get back in with your badge."

I locked up and headed to lunch with Syeer. There were a few other people here, but I didn't know them enough to speak. Syeer introduced us and we grabbed our food and sat down. I was expecting to see people side-eyeing us, but everyone minded their own business.

"How long you been married?" Syeer broke the silence.

"About seven years."

"Now, that's relationship goals."

"Thank you." I smiled.

"I'm serious. I can't wait to get married and have a house full of kids."

"I thought for sure you were married," I said.

"No, not me. I've tried dating, but most of the women think I'm soft or they want money. Once they date me and see what type of man I am, they usually run for the hills."

"What type of man are you?" I quizzed. I didn't know what had made me ask him that.

"I believe in chivalry. I like dates and taking care of my woman, but also letting her be independent as well. I believe in communicating with her and making sure we are both happy in the relationship. I don't ever want to be happy and she's feeling some type of way. Women are strange creatures and I enjoy learning about y'all. Y'all can love us so hard even through our mistakes. Some men wise up and grow up and some continue on until that woman is long gone and he doesn't even know it because y'all still fight through it."

Everything Syeer was saying was hitting home for me. I was almost at the point of tears as he sat there and continued to talk. I grabbed a napkin and stopped the tear that tried to fall from my eye.

"Are you okay?"

"My allergies. I'm sorry, what were you saying?"

"I've talked enough. Let's get back to work. I really enjoyed lunch with you. Maybe tomorrow I'll let you educate me on how to get a woman." He laughed.

"Yea, I guess I could help."

The rest of my day was pretty decent. I finished all my paperwork and turned it in, and tomorrow, I would be starting fresh on my first marketing campaign, and I was so excited.

Syeer walked me down to my car because I parked so far down. I didn't want to take someone's parking spot and get chewed out, so I opted to park out of the way.

"You have a good night, Cori."

"You too, Syeer."

I headed home and the stuff Syeer had said earlier was running through my head. I wanted to go home and confront Mari on his affair and start fresh. It wasn't like I was going to leave him; where would I go? I couldn't go back to my parents. I could, but I didn't want to. I didn't like people in my business. I suffered in silence a lot of the time. I had to be strong. Strong was all I knew. I was a black woman and we were raised to put it on our back and keep moving. I pulled up to the house with a massive headache and walked over to the neighbor's house to get Kj.

After I had helped Kj with his homework, I ordered some pizza and put some up for Mari. I couldn't be mad at him. Maybe I wasn't what he wanted right now. Maybe I needed to get off his back about having a baby. I showered and climbed into the bed. It was around one in the morning before I was finally able to go to sleep. The chime of the alarm system woke me out of my sleep. I had looked at the time before Mari walked in the room. I watched him as he kicked his shoes off and walked into the bathroom. The scent of a woman filled our room. I heard the shower turn on as I laid there, fighting the tears. I'd had enough already. I threw the cover off and entered the bathroom.

"You washing her off you?" I stood there with my arms crossed.

"What you talking about, baby?" Mari continued to wash himself behind the glass door.

"The woman you just left. I smelled her on you when you walked in the room. Are you cheating on me, Mari?"

"Girl, you're delusional. No, I'm not cheating on you. Go get back in the bed and get some rest."

I couldn't believe he was going to lie to my face. I debated with my reality. My husband was a liar and a cheater. I snatched the glass door open as he washed his hair.

"Mari, you're lying and I know for a fact you're lying. I saw you in H&M the other day. I heard everything you told her about me. Do you want me to tell you what she looks like?"

He was like a deer caught in headlights. I stormed off before he saw me cry. My feelings were hurt because he had lied. I never thought he would do this. He came out the bathroom with soap still dripping off him.

"Cori, now you know I would never do anything to hurt you. I'm so sorry, I messed up. She doesn't mean nothing to me."

"Just shut up, Mari. You lied to me. If she's what you want, why the hell you here?" I eyed him.

"I don't want to be with her. Look, you were on some bull. You always do the same thing over and over again, nagging me about a baby and all that other stuff. I need room to breathe."

"So, it's my fault you cheated? Get out my face before I snap, Mari."

"It's my fault, but I'm just telling you what the problem was."

"You don't think I have problems with you? You don't think I get tired of sitting around here, cooking and cleaning after you and Kj? You never ask how I feel about anything!" I yelled.

"I'm going to the man cave because obviously, you're upset and I don't want to wake Kj up."

"No, how about you go back to where you came from."

"I'm not leaving you."

"Well, I'll leave then."

"Cori, you can't be serious right now. It's almost four in the morning. You are not about to leave this house with that boy, a'ight? I'll leave."

Mari packed a small bag as I sat on the side of the bed, fighting back my tears. He grabbed the bag and kissed me on my forehead. When I heard the door close, I broke down. My

55

heart was broken to pieces. I couldn't have children, and now I had to share my husband with another woman. I cried so much until I was sick to my stomach. I crawled into the bed and covered myself up. My room door opened and Kj walked in. I wiped my face as he got into bed with me and rubbed my back. Kj was a special child. Whenever he was around, the energy changed. He laid his head on my pillow.

"I love you, auntie."

"I love you, too, nephew. Now, go to sleep because you got school in the morning."

No matter how I felt, Kj's well-being was my priority over my own.

The next morning, I was up, getting Kj ready for school when Mari walked in the door. He must've called out from work. I didn't care either way it went; I was going to work. I still hadn't told him.

"Why you dressed up?" Mari asked me.

"I got a job," I replied without looking at him.

I kissed Kj as he ran off with my neighbor. I had waved at her and her son before I went back in the house to finish getting ready. Mari followed me from the room to the bathroom and I ignored him until I grabbed my purse.

"When were you going to tell me?"

"When were you going to tell me I was old fashion and you were cheating on me?"

That shut him right up. I got my stuff and walked out the door. I was looking forward to talking to Syeer today. I had a lot to tell him about treating a woman right, something my husband used to do, but stopped doing when he started letting other things occupy his time.

I parked a little closer today. Again, Syeer had coffee sitting on my desk. I thought the gesture was so sweet, but my mind was on the events from last night. Deep down, I knew Mari loved me. It was in his eyes when he looked at me, but something was still pulling his heart away from me.

"Good morning." Syeer peeked in.

"Good morning."

"Are you okay?"

"Yea, I'm fine."

"You look different from yesterday."

"Really?"

"Not in a bad way. Let me rephrase that. You're not wearing your glasses, for one."

"I forgot them, but I have contacts in, just for today," I told him.

"Well, you look good either way. Welp, today you get your first task. Are you ready and focused?"

Did he say I looked good?

"Yes, I'm ready and focused," I replied.

"Okay, so I stayed up all last night coming up with some type of slogan for this makeup company. I'm not big on stuff like this, so I'm hoping we can put our heads together and come up with something dope. It's urban so we can put our own spin on it."

He gave me the pictures and the slogan and I was kind of feeling it. I thought it was cute, coming from a man's perspective. All I had to do was tweak it a little to grab a woman's attention. I changed a few things in his original slogan and showed him my changes.

"Wow! You got me wanting to buy makeup for a woman and I ain't got one." He laughed.

"Don't flatter me."

"No, seriously, you should've been working."

"Okay, so what's next?" I asked.

"We wait, once we send this off. We can start on the hard part now and that's reaching out to potentials who may be interested in trying it for the magazine and getting a few models in to add to the advertisement."

"That's not hard. That's the fun part," I stated.

"I'm about to go to my office and send you the stuff. You can look over it and start if you're comfortable. You're doing a great job so far."

"Thank you."

As soon as Syeer walked out and closed my door, my phone started ringing in my purse. I dug in it to answer it.

"Hello?" I juggled with the phone.

"Mrs. Carter, this is Kenny's teacher. He got into an accident here at school. He's fine, but I wanted to make you aware that he did fall and bump his head."

"Oh, thank you for calling me."

"But, Mrs. Carter, I do have some concerns. He had a bruise on his back. Are you aware of how it got there?"

"No, ma'am. It wasn't there last night. He does bruise easily, obviously." I chuckled.

"He states he doesn't know how it got there either. I know how attentive you are and I don't want to report it, but if the wrong person sees it, then it's out of my hands. Could you talk to him about it and see what he says?"

"Thank you for doing this. I'll never do anything to hurt him."

"I know, and that's why I wanted to talk to you. Have a good day, Mrs. Carter."

"You too."

I couldn't focus on my work because I was concerned about Kj. The only person he was with was my neighbor. I was going to talk to them once I left here. I needed answers. I looked over what Syeer had sent and even skipped lunch to get it done. I didn't bother Syeer all day and he didn't really bother me. He would check on me, but that was about it. By the end of the day, I was out the door so fast, no one knew I was gone.

Mari's car was parked in the same spot it was in this morning, but that wasn't my concern right now. I got out of the car and headed towards my neighbor's house. I beat on the door and Kj ran to the door with his book bag on.

"Oh, hey."

"What happened to his back?" I asked my neighbor.

"The boys were tussling in the backseat this morning and my son pushed him into the door."

"So, you knew he had a bruise on him and didn't think it was important enough to let me know? You have my number. All it takes is a simple phone call."

"But—"

"Don't 'but' me. Kj means the world to me, and if it were your son, I would've called you."

Kj was pulling my hand towards the house, but I had a lot of anger built up. Maybe I was releasing it on the wrong person, but I didn't care. I could tell she was shocked by my actions by the look on her face. I let Kj lead the way as I placed my key in the door and was amazed at how clean the house was, and I could smell food.

"Hey, Kj, I'll see you in the game before you go to bed. Go put your stuff up so you can eat," Mari told him, before turning his attention to me.

He kissed my lips and pulled me in for a hug.

"I got the floors waxed and dinner ready for you. I want to hear about your day."

"I appreciate that. Any help around here helps," I told him.

He took my purse and put it up. Kj was back and we all gathered around the table to enjoy dinner. We were back to how it was supposed to be. I smiled at my boys and hoped it lasted.

Paris

I had been in Brazil for two months now. I snuck back into the States to grab some things and left the very next day. Cori called me several times a week until I finally got my number changed. I thought it was no big deal until today. Novi was acting strangely towards me. He was staying out later than usual after his games. I would go and show my face and put on a pretty smile, but I was so unhappy. There were clothes and shoes piling up in my closet, cars overflowing outside and my bank account had caught the holy ghost, but still, I was empty. I missed my son and Cori. The sense of having someone who cared for you was pulling at me today.

"I really need you to take it easy. You're stressing about something and it's causing your blood pressure to go up. You know how important this baby is to Novi, right?"

"Yes, I do."

"Okay, so rest."

Novi's personal doctor left the house and I was alone again. I was put on strict bed rest, so I wasn't able to make it to Novi's game tonight. I could've watched it on television, but I still hadn't learned their language. I got up to go to the bathroom. I finished and washed my hands and looked at myself in the mirror. Even my appearance had changed. I was still pretty, but money had changed me. My brows were tattooed on and my five-hundred-dollar hair was switched for thousand-dollar hair. I went and climbed back in bed and flipped the television on just to look at the game.

My phone buzzed and it was a text from Novi telling me to be dressed by 11 tonight. Since I was at the beginning of my pregnancy, I was extremely tired. I had no idea where we could be going that late at night. I didn't respond, and when he got here, I was going to be asleep. I wanted to go home for a few weeks just to feel normal again. At halftime, Novi had scored thirty-one points and they were up by ten. I turned everything off and fell asleep.

"Paris, Novi is waiting for you in the car," the helper stated.

I reached over on the nightstand and called his phone.

"Are you ready, beautiful?"

"I'm sleeping, Novi. You know I'm on bed rest," I complained.

"Paris, you signed up for this, and I really need you tonight. This party is very important to me." Novi always brought up the fact that I had signed the agreement. Whenever he did that, there was no need to argue.

I hung up the phone with an attitude and flung the covers off me. I searched the massive closet for something to wear that wouldn't show my small stomach that was forming. Novi wanted to save the news until I was at least five or six months. I selected a red sequin Versace dress that hung off my shoulders a little and diamond heels. I unwrapped my hair and ran my fingers through the curls. I washed my face and brushed my teeth before I applied light makeup. I threw on gloss and was out the door in twenty minutes tops.

I climbed into the car and my head was instantly snapped back from the hard slap to the mouth Novi had given me. My lip was split from his championship ring and all I saw was the deep red blood dripping on my expensive dress. Maybe Novi didn't know me as well as he thought he did. I was hood, real hood. I started clawing at his face and throwing punches left and right. His Porsche was so small; he couldn't get me off him. I was hitting Novi so hard that my wrist was starting to hurt. The passenger side door was pulled open and I was pulled off Novi and into the house as I heard his tires screeching in our circular driveway.

"Has he lost his mind putting his hands on me?" I snatched away from Novi's security, Tommy.

"Calm down," Tommy said in a hushed tone.

"Don't tell me to calm down, Tommy. Ain't no man on this earth going to ever put their hands on me and get away with it.

Don't you ever tell a black woman to calm down. Ever!" I paced the floor.

Tommy walked off without saying anything else. I stormed up to our room and looked for my phone, but everything was in the car with Novi. I hated him. I hated this whole agreement we had come up with. I pulled off my clothes and put back on my pajama set, then went into the bathroom to look at my face. It wasn't as bad as I thought it was. My lip was still busted, but I was sure Novi was somewhere looking worse than me. I washed the blood from my lip and took a Tylenol and went to bed.

♥

The sound of the birds chirping was my wake-up call. Novi hadn't come home last night and I was starting to think this was going to be the beginning of a messy situation. I threw my legs over the bed and noticed my purse. I grabbed it and searched through it for my phone. I contemplated calling Cori just to hear her voice, but Novi walking into the room distracted me. His face was scratched up badly.

"I need you dressed and ready within an hour," he said before walking off.

I wasn't in the mood to do any smiling and fronting when we were not on good terms. My body was so sore from last night. From what he had on, I didn't have to dress up, so that was a good thing. I got dressed and was downstairs where Novi was waiting, looking at his watch. He opened the door for me to walk out first. He still hadn't spoken about last night and I didn't know where we were going. He could've been taking me to get killed for all I know.

"I think I got out of hand last night. I don't really do stuff like that. I think losing our first game of this season did something to me and I totally lost it. Forgive me for hurting you and my unborn child. To make it up to you, I would like to start over and go out to dinner with you."

"Apology accepted."

"You really jumped on me, though. I've never been beat up by a woman." Novi laughed.

"I don't play them type of games. You forgot I'm from the hood?"

"I must've forgot who you were."

We enjoyed dinner and conversation, which was something we hadn't done since my first week here. Novi slid a box across the table to me and I looked at him, waiting for an explanation of what was in the box.

"It's a gift. I feel bad about last night."

I opened the box and it was a diamond necklace. I know this set him back a few hundred thousand.

"May I ask where you get this kind of money? I googled your salary and it's nothing compared to what LeBron or an American player makes."

He leaned down so only I could hear him.

"You googled my salary? Paris, you just keep disappointing me. I'm trying to be patient with you. You ever heard what happens when you go digging for stuff? I suggest you don't go digging, baby. You're going to find something you may not want to see."

I closed the box and pushed it back toward him. Novi looked at me strangely before he looked around the restaurant and put the box in his jacket pocket. We got dessert and ate it in silence. I wasn't sure what Novi was implying, but I was sure going to find out. I always wondered why he never came back home after he left. He had a thing for Brazil, but before Brazil, he was in Panama. Novi had some secrets and I was about to be Inspector Gadget.

"I'll be going home for a few days next week." I finally spoke up once we were in the car.

"You cannot go back home, Paris. I thought I made myself clear in the contract. That's no longer your life."

"It's my father's birthday."

"Well, give him a call. You're not traveling with my child, and aren't you on bed rest?" he reminded me.

To keep from arguing, I left the situation alone. We were back home, and I decided to call my parents for a change. No one knew about my new number, and I was at the point of breaking down. While Novi took a shower, I stepped out on the balcony for some privacy.

"Hey, mommy, it's Paris," I said before she hung up.

"Paris, is this really you? Girl, I've been going crazy and your daddy has been ready to slap the black off you. If it wasn't for Cori telling us where you were, I would've done a missing person report."

"I'm fine, mommy. I'm married and pregnant."

"Say what now?"

"Yea, you heard me right."

"I don't know whether to be happy or upset. Your daddy is going to be pissed."

"I know. I wanted to surprise him, but my blood pressure has been high, so I've been put on bed rest."

"Is your husband stressing you?"

"Paris?" Novi called out to me.

"Is that him?" my mother asked.

"Mommy, I've got to go. I'll call y'all back. Love you," I said before hanging up.

I knew Novi wanted sex. It was routine. Every other day, I laid down and let Novi do what he wanted. He requested that I not move or make any sounds. While he was the only one benefiting from this relationship, I wanted out. He forbade me from looking over the contract so I couldn't look for any loopholes. He did his business as I stared off into space. I did anything to detach myself from my reality. When he was done, he kissed me, which was always the most passionate part of the marriage.

"Come shower with me."

I rolled my eyes in the back of my head. I just wanted to be left alone at this point.

"Can't I please just lay here? I'm not feeling good," I lied.

Novi got up to take his shower and I ran to the other room to take a quick wash off before he got out the shower. When he got out, I was already asleep. I woke up to him rubbing my stomach and kissing my shoulder. I guess everything that glitters ain't gold.

One month later…

Novi had missed another doctor's appointment due to practice. The temperature outside was muggy and I was in a very bad mood. The doctor relieved me from bed rest and I was able to move around freely. Novi had never allowed me to go to a real doctor. Instead, he called one of the doctors over to the house to see about me. I wasn't too sure he knew anything about pregnant women and their hormones.

Novi had at least four games left, but he had to travel for his next game, so I made plans to get out a little and explore while he was gone. He was leaving out tomorrow and coming home on Monday. I had his bags packed and ready, so all he had to do was grab them and leave.

I wasn't ready to go home yet, so I swung by the store and grabbed some of my favorite cupcakes from the local bakery and some fresh fruit. I was now four months and a small pouch was forming at the bottom of my stomach. We had another month before we revealed to the public that we were pregnant. From the spreading of my hips and the widening of my nose, any normal person would be able to see, but everyone was so into themselves in the places I hung out that it was easy to just blend in.

By the time I had made it home, Novi's bags were gone. A part of me was glad that I had missed him. I put my stuff up in the kitchen and walked to Novi's office. Today was my lucky day because he had left it unlocked. Knowing him, it was a trap set up for me, but I was going to find that contract and our marriage license. Before walking in, I looked around to make sure no one saw me slip in. I eased the door shut and locked it. Usually, his office didn't look like this, but there were papers scattered everywhere.

"Where did he put it?" I shifted some of the papers on his desk.

I saw a few bank statements, but there was nothing to be alarmed about. I then started pulling at the drawers, but they were locked. This had to be where it was. I started searching for the key until it dawned on me that he kept it around his neck until he showered. I was defeated. I flopped down in his office chair and cried. This by far was one of the dumbest things I had ever done.

"Did someone come in here?" I heard Novi ask.

My heart started racing as I looked for somewhere to hide. The office was the size of a living room, so my options were plenty. I only had a few seconds, but I made it in between his sofa and wall before the door burst open. I had to cover my mouth because I was breathing so hard. My heart was beating so fast that it had my shirt moving to the rhythm and my blood pressure was rising because the room was starting to spin.

"I've got to find that paper. I have a flight leaving in less than an hour. Why do I pay you to organize these things and you don't know where you put something?" Novi fussed.

I wanted to see who he paid to organize his office, but I didn't want to chance them seeing me.

"Novi, I don't remember you giving it to me. I remember everything, trust me. I have the memory of an elephant and that's why you brought me on."

"Are you saying I'm lying?" Novi asked.

"No, I would never—"

A gunshot went off, followed by a thud. I thought I had given myself away when a noise slipped out, but the shot was so loud, it could be heard down the block. Novi didn't have neighbors, though, so it didn't matter.

"Tommy, come take the trash out."

Tommy's heavy footsteps could be heard walking towards the office.

"Where to?"

"Just chop her up and have her delivered to her parents' house in a trash bag. I want her family to at least have a burial for her. Have you seen Paris around here? Her car is out front."

"No, I haven't seen her."

I prayed to the Most High that He didn't start looking for me. I was terrified. Who was Novi Warren? Right now, he looked like a murderer. The sound of the body dragging across the hardwood floor made me sick to my stomach. Novi was still in the office and I couldn't move, but I was balled up in an awkward position. Because of the small ball that was forming in my stomach, it was hard for me to sit still in the small space I had crawled in. He slammed something shut and walked out. I had waited for another fifteen minutes before I came out of my hiding spot.

I had to get out of his office before I got caught. I walked past his desk but backed up when I noticed a key. I looked up at the door before I grabbed the key and placed it in my bra. The pool of blood that was at the door brought vomit up and I ran to the trash can and released it, then wiped my mouth with the back of my hand. I slipped out of his office, making sure to leave it unlocked so I could get back in.

It was close to four in the morning and I couldn't sleep. Novi had called to check on me when he landed, but we only talked briefly before he had to go. He extended his time, and instead of coming back Monday, he wouldn't be back until Tuesday, so I booked a flight home for a few days. I didn't tell anyone because I wanted to surprise everyone. I planned on being back on Monday and I had to pay the staff to leave for the week. I would deal with Novi when he got back. I didn't need staff here while I was gone. I was going to leave my car, so if someone stopped by, they would think I was here.

I packed and threw all my stuff by the door. I pulled the key out of my pocket and entered Novi's office again. I placed the key in the drawer and it unlocked. My breathing changed as

I pulled it open. I thumbed through the files labeled by name, but I didn't know any of them.

"What are you doing in my house?"

I slammed the drawer closed, but not before pulling my file. Standing before me was a very handsome male. His lashes and brows were manicured and his nails were very clean. He wasn't a manly man; he was very feminine.

"Did you hear what I asked you?"

"I'm sorry, I didn't get your name?"

"I don't have to tell you who I am. You're in my house and in my man's office. He never lets anyone in here."

"Excuse me, did you say your man?" I asked.

"Oh, my goodness." He flicked his bang back with his middle finger. "Don't tell me Novi done brought another dumb female in my house. I told him that the next time this happened, we were through."

"You know what, I'm actually about to leave. You won't have to worry about me ever again."

I grabbed my file and walked past him. He smelled very good but I kept my good eye on him just in case he felt the need to swing. I had never fought a dude like him before but I was sure I could take him.

"I'm tired of y'all coming in here, thinking y'all can do what y'all want. I bet he gave you a card, too, didn't he?"

"I'm not obligated to tell you that."

"I bet I'll be obligated to drag you in this office if you don't answer me," he said.

"Wait a minute. I think you're taking your anger out on the wrong person. The only dragging going on in here is me dragging you by that weave. Don't disrespect me because I haven't been disrespectful to you.

He slipped out of his shoes and threw his man bag down, then hopped around like he was ready to box me out. I couldn't help but burst out laughing.

"Look here, bruh, I can't take you serious. I got a flight to catch. Tell my husband if he wants to see his unborn child or me again to give me a call," I stated before walking past him.

I made it to the foyer to grab my bags and made my mind up that I wasn't coming back. It all made sense why the room I stayed in when I arrived was full of male clothes. Novi was bisexual and had used me as a cover up. I planned on making it back to the States and paying my bills up for a year before Novi deactivated all my cards. I was holding on to the most precious cargo inside my stomach. It was my meal ticket.

Mari

Terreka was my world. I thought I would never find love outside of Cori until Terreka birthed our first child. Yesterday, I watched my daughter enter the world. Cori was so naïve. She was hating on the wrong girl. The chick she had seen me in the store with was a female friend. Did I sleep with her? You have to know I smashed a few times, but we both knew it was nothing serious.

"Isn't she beautiful?" Terreka rubbed our daughter's curly hair as she breast fed her.

"Beautiful just like you. Thank you for giving me such a gorgeous baby." I kissed her forehead.

"How is this going to work now? Do I still patiently wait, or are we moving forward?"

"We moving forward. I'm telling Cori tonight."

Terreka cried tears of joys. She had played second most of my marriage. At first, I wasn't sure what I felt for Terreka. I met her right after Cori and I got married and she had lost the first baby. She was having a hard time grabbing something off the top shelf at the grocery store when I went to pick up something for Cori. I helped her out but never got her name. I knew it was destiny when I ran into her again with a flat tire. We exchanged numbers and started sneak texting. I was blunt with her and she was aware of Cori. Then, I had no intentions of leaving my wife. After all the miscarriages, the love dwindled.

I hated to even think about breaking Cori's heart. She had a heart of gold, but we were better off as friends. Our marriage was over. Terreka and my daughter, Majesty, were all that I needed. Then, the thought of Kj hit me. He was a part of my world. I had raised him with Cori since he had come home from the hospital. It broke my heart that I was about to hurt him. All his life, people he loved had walked out. I looked over at Terreka and she was fast asleep with Majesty on her chest. I kissed both of them and headed out.

I sat in the car, pondering my thoughts. The rain was beating down on my car and the sky was turning purple from the lightning. The lights were on in the house and I was late for dinner after I had promised Cori I would be here on time. She thought everything was on point, but I had only been nice these last four months for this moment. This was going to be the hardest thing for me to do. A part of me wanted to make it all go away and be a family man to both of them, but Cori couldn't give me what I wanted the most. When she begged me to go to the doctor, Terreka was already pregnant, so I knew I wasn't the problem.

I finally got out of the car. Running up to the door, I opened it and the smell of food hit me like a ton of bricks. Cori cooked like somebody's grandma and I loved that about her. Cori was at the table with her laptop and papers spread out as she stuffed her face with food. Since she had started working, this had become her life. She still took care of Kj and me, but work was her priority. I, for one, hated for a woman to work but I didn't argue or push the issue with her.

"Hey, I didn't hear you come in. Are you hungry?" she asked, taking her glasses off.

Cori was cute, but Terreka was fine. Cori rubbed her eyes and placed her glasses back on her face before she got out of the chair and started fixing my plate.

"Cori, sit down, I need to talk to you."

"Is everything okay?" She placed the plate down and gave me her full attention.

"My girl had a baby yesterday," I blurted out.

"Wha-what did you just say?" her voice trembled. "Your girl? What girl, Mari? Is it the girl from the store? You told me it was just me, you and Kj." She started crying.

"No, it's not her. I'm sorry, baby, I really am. I didn't mean to do you this way, but I knew you would never be able to have a baby."

The same plate she was fixing for me came flying towards me. I didn't move in time. The plate broke right above my head, but not without cutting me across my cheek, leaving a big gash. I blacked out. I wrapped my hands around Cori's neck and picked her small frame up from the floor. I could feel her life slipping through my fingers, but as her clawing got weaker, her wedding ring caught the light and I released she was still my wife. She slipped down to the floor, gasping for air. My face was burning and the thick, dark blood was staining my shirt. I stared at her and asked myself how I had even let things get this far.

"Don't leave like this, Mari," Cori cried out.

Kj came running into the kitchen.

"Go to your room, Kj!" I yelled.

He took off running and his door slammed. Cori was finally up off the floor, facing me. Seeing how far things had gone tonight, hurt me. My phone started ringing in my pocket. This was not the right time for Terreka to call.

"Is that her?" Cori asked with venom dripping from her lips.

I didn't answer her. Instead, I walked to our room to start packing.

"Answer me, Mari! I'm still your wife. You at least owe me an explanation."

"Cori, I don't have an explanation. I fell in love and I can't help it. Let me go so I can go get my face checked." I snatched the two suitcases off the bed.

"You love her?" Cori asked, but I didn't answer.

It was like I had knocked the breath out of her. I wasn't going to make it worse. I took my key off my keychain, threw it on the table and walked out. Once our emotions were in check, I would come back and holler at her. She was still my wife, and I didn't plan on divorcing her anytime soon. It was bad enough I had just walked out on her; I didn't want to make it worse by forcing her to divorce me. I threw the suitcases in the trunk as Kj stared at me from his window. I couldn't stare at him long because his little face held hurt and anger. When I got into the car, I could see Cori grabbing him and closing the curtain. I really felt like a piece of me had been ripped from my body. I started my car and headed back towards the hospital. I had to get my face looked at before I went back to Terreka's room.

Six staples later, I was approaching Terreka's door with balloons and a bear. I just wanted to hold my daughter and go to sleep.

"Mari, what happened to your face?" Terreka asked.

"I'm fine. Cori and I had a little fight."

"I'm sorry it had to end this way. I never wanted to break up your home."

"Don't stress about it. What's done is done, and now we can move forward with our family," I told her.

This was going to be easier said than done. My world was about to change and I was hoping for the better.

Cori

I balled up in bed and shivered and cried until I was sick to my stomach. I had put all my faith in Mari. I trusted him with my heart and this was what he did to me. I had never done anything outside of our marriage. I loved him unconditionally, and even with him walking out on me, I still loved him and would take him back right now. I had work in a few hours and I still couldn't seem to fall asleep. The last four months had been blissful for us. He came home for dinner since his hours had gone back to normal and he wasn't hanging out late. What had I done wrong? I just knew we were on track. We were even having sex again. If you would've asked me if I thought my husband had another life, I would've looked you in your eyes and told you no.

How was I supposed to go on with my life? Mari provided everything for me. We had built this house together and now I was alone. I rolled over to look on his side of the bed and anger consumed me. I grabbed my phone and called him over and over again. I didn't care about his new girlfriend having a new baby. I was his wife. How dare he just walk into our home and tell me it was over between us. His phone rang the first five times I had called, and now it was going to voicemail. I called the hospital to see if I could get some information, but they couldn't give me anything. Was I bitter? Nah! I was mad as hell.

I got out of bed and threw on some jeans and a shirt and got Kj ready as well. He was still asleep, so I carried him to the car. We got in the car and headed to the hospital. I couldn't get out and ask any questions that I didn't know the answers to, so I planned on waiting as long as I had to for him to come out. Kj started to stir in his sleep around six. His body was used to getting up and going to school, so it took me forever to get him to go to sleep. He wanted to know what was going on with his Uncle Mari but I didn't have an answer. I couldn't make Mari look bad in Kj's eyes. He had raised Kj and he was the only man Kj knew.

I started the car to get some cool air circulating. I looked back and forth from my clock to Mari's car. I had to leave in thirty minutes if I was going to make it home to get Kj ready for school.

"Please come out. Please come out. I know you're going home today," I said out loud.

I had parked a row over from Mari's car. The hospital was huge, so I couldn't see the entrance, but having an eye on his car was all I needed. I looked at the clock again and I was officially late getting Kj ready for school. It was now 7:15 in the morning and I was still stalking my husband. It had consumed me. I always kept a bag in the car for emergencies, so I could still get him to school on time if they would just come out. I wanted to see her. The woman in me wanted to know who she was and how she looked. Was she prettier than me? Was she taller than me? Was she thick? What was it that made my husband leave his home to be with her?

I gave up. I put the car in drive with tears in my eyes. I was hurting so bad, I couldn't even see the road in front of me. I covered my mouth to keep myself from screaming and scaring my nephew. I wiped my face with the back of my hand as I pulled up in Paris' driveway since her place was closer to the hospital. I got Kj Pop-Tarts ready while he brushed his teeth and got dressed.

My eyes were swollen and my body was weak, but I got him to school and drove home to get myself ready.

"Hey, beau—" Syeer burst into my office.

I wiped my eyes with a Kleenex.

"Whoa, what's wrong with you?" he asked, concerned.

"I'm good." I released a half-smile.

"Nah, you ain't good. You've been here four months and I've seen you good, and this ain't it."

I couldn't talk to another man about my marriage. What if I took my husband back? I couldn't make him look bad. I finished cleaning my face and straightened myself up.

"I'm fine. I didn't get a chance to finish our project last night, but I promise to have it done before I leave today, even if I have to stay late."

"Cori, we'll work on it together. I'm not sure what's going on, but don't ever think I'll take the information you give me and run with it. I know what hurt feels like."

"Trust me, Syeer, I'm good."

"A'ight, well, let's get to work then."

Syeer stayed by my side as we worked on the project I was in the middle of doing when Mari broke the news to me. We finished it around lunch time and I was now sitting across from Syeer, enjoying a hefty serving of oxtails and cabbage at his family's Jamaican restaurant.

"I told you food always makes you feel better."

"This is really good. I don't even think I cook oxtails this good."

"I'm just glad to see you smiling," he told me.

"Thank you for just giving me space. Most people would've pestered me into telling them what was wrong."

"I'm not one of them. If you ever need to talk, though, I'm here."

I replied with a smile. We headed back to the office and finished our day. I picked Kj up from my parents' house and tried not to get out of the car, but my father came to the door and waved me in. I got myself together before I walked in. If Kj had told them about last night, I was going to kill him.

"Hey, daddy." I tiptoed to kiss his jaw.

He carried a look of concern on his face.

"Paris came and got Kj."

"Daddy, why the heck would you let her do that?"

"Because he is her son. I know many people don't know the secret, not even her own parents, but let her keep him sometimes. Besides, you need a break to focus on your own marriage. Kj told me Mari packed two suitcases and left last night."

"I swear I'm going to kill him."

"No, you're not. Now, what's going on?"

"We'll be fine, daddy, trust me."

"If you say so, but if you can't handle it, then I can. I got something to burn a hole in him. Don't think I don't see those marks around your neck. You do a terrible job at hiding stuff, Cori."

I held my head down from embarrassment. My daddy had a terrible issue with his anger. Once he turned green, it was hard for him to turn brown again. I didn't want my husband and father fighting.

"I got to go and find out where Paris and Kj went. Tell Mama I love her."

I ran out the house before he could say anything else. My daddy wasn't just making empty threats. He was serious about handling Mari if he needed to. I hated being in the middle of this mess, but right now, my concern was Kj and Paris. She didn't even tell me she was coming back into town. I preferred to prep Kj before his encounters with his mother. He was old enough to know certain things, but I always told him that his mother loved him. I would never taint his relationship with his mother. I pulled up in front of Paris' house and got out.

"I knew you would be over here after a while. I was just telling Kj we better hurry up and finish dinner." Paris smiled at me from the door.

"Why didn't you call me and tell me you were coming home?" I quizzed.

"I wanted to surprise y'all."

"Are you okay? You look a little swollen?"

"Can you at least get in the house before you start doing your observation of me, please?"

I walked in and could smell the food. Paris wasn't a big cook, so I immediately went to the kitchen to assist her with whatever it was she was making. Kj was sitting at the table on the iPad. I walked up to him and kissed him on the top of his head and he looked up and smiled and that was all I needed. I walked back to where Paris was standing. She looked confused about how much milk to add to the cornbread, so I took it from her and did it myself.

"You want to tell me why you snuck back in? We talk about everything. You blocked me from calling you and now several months later, here you are."

Paris looked at Kj and pulled my arm towards the living room. She was taller than me, so, of course, I was stumbling, trying to keep my feet under me. Whatever she had to say must've been important. She had no filter around Kj any other time, so I wondered what was really going on.

"I'm pregnant, Cori."

"Excuse me? What did you just say, Paris?"

"I went to Brazil, married Novi, and now I'm pregnant with his child."

"Paris, how stupid can you be? Okay, so how far along are you?"

"I'm a few months."

"And what does Novi have to say about all of this? Where is he, anyway?"

"It's a long story and I don't want to get into it right now."

"I respect that," I told Paris.

I had my own issues and I didn't really have time to get into hers. When she was ready to talk about it, she would.

"Do you at least plan on taking care of this child?" I asked.

"How dare you ask me that? If you're having a problem taking care of Kj, I'll get my son and do it myself."

"Why are you getting an attitude? I just asked. I have the right to ask that, being that you already have one you're not taking care of," I stated.

"You know what, get out my house. You really think you're better than me, don't you? But, you can't keep your husband to yourself. I've been trying to tell you for the longest he was cheating on you. Yea, he treats you good, but he's a dog and will always be a dog. I hate females like you. You ain't 'bout nothing. I'll keep my son, and I'll call you when I'm ready for you to see him," Paris explained as she pushed me towards the door.

Before I could say anything to her, she had slammed the door in my face. I pulled my phone out to call her, but she didn't answer. She didn't have the patience to keep Kj more than two days, so I got in my car and headed home. This was going to be my first night at home without my husband. I was still hurting and wanted to know what the woman looked like until I pulled up to the house and noticed Mari's car. I rushed and got out of the car and went into the house.

When I walked in, Mari was sitting on the sofa on his phone. The television was off and the house was quiet. A chill went down my spine. I couldn't take anything else at the moment. I dropped my purse and keys and walked towards him. I wanted to kiss him, hug him and beg him to come home. He looked up from his phone and gave me a saddened look as he put his phone in his pocket and stood up.

"Hey," he said lowly.

"Hey."

"I stopped by to check on you. I feel bad about what happened to us. I wanted to see if you needed anything. I made sure the bills were paid for the month and stocked the refrigerator. Is Kj all right?" He looked around.

"Yea, he's with Paris."

I walked into the kitchen to fix myself something to eat. Seeing Mari was making me sick, just knowing he was going to walk out the door and go back to his family after he left me.

"Cori, we don't have to hate each other. I'm still going to be here for you and Kj. I'm still your husband."

"That's funny, Mari. You're right, you are still *my* husband, but you found the time to crawl in between the legs of another woman with no protection and start a whole family. I'm assuming she knows you're here with your wife?" I eyed him, but he never answered. "I guess she doesn't know. If I can remember correctly, you dropped your key on the table and left last night. Now, I would like for you to leave the spare key and walk out the door and never come back unless you want your marriage. I'm not about to compete with another woman."

"But—" He tried to talk.

"Mari, seriously, you've hurt me enough, don't you think? Just leave and let me move on. Thank you for everything, but I got it from here on out. Focus on taking care of the family you've started."

Mari walked towards me and wrapped me in his arms and I didn't stop him. I was mad, but the touch of my husband was still familiar to me. It was all I ever knew. Mari rested his chin on top my head as I laid my head on his chest and listened to his heart beat. It was funny how the same sound I fell in love with was now breaking my heart. I thought our hearts were intertwined, but a strange woman broke up what I thought was mine.

"I'm sorry, Cori. I love you so much."

I silently let the tears run from my eyes. I desperately wanted to tell him I loved him too, but my heart wouldn't let me. Once we released each other, this was the end. I unwrapped my hands from Mari's back and attempted to walk away, but

Mari wouldn't let me. He picked me up bridal style and toted me to our room and laid me down on the bed, stripping me out of my clothes. I nervously watched as he took his clothes off and climbed into bed. He planted kisses all over me and I was confused about what we were doing. I didn't have the time to question him, so I let him have his way. He was technically still mine so what we were doing was practically fine.

"Mari?" I walked around the house wrapped in a sheet, looking for him.

It was only eight in the morning and the weekend had just started for me. I thought I was going to wake up to my husband, but there was no evidence he had even been here. I fought the tears that formed in my eyes. I grabbed my phone to call Mari and he picked up on the first ring.

"What's up, Cori?"

"What's up? Why didn't you wake me up?"

"You were sleeping peacefully. I didn't want to bother you."

"Where are you right now?"

He didn't have to answer because I could hear a soft cry in the background. I held the phone to my ear as I slid down the wall. My lips trembled as the female's voice softly quieted her baby.

"You need something?" Mari broke the silence.

"When will you be back?" I asked.

"I'm not coming back. I thought I told you that."

"Mari, don't do this to me, please. I thought last night was…was—"

"I got to go, Cori."

The line went dead and I was left to comfort myself.

Nothing made me feel better than a nice glass of Jack Daniels.

Mari

Hearing Cori crying broke my heart. I felt so bad, but I had Terreka grilling me the whole time I was on the phone. She had no idea I was with Cori last night. I had told her I was going to hang out with a few of my boys just to get a breather. Jumping from one situation to another was taking a toll on me and it had only been a day, but I missed my wife.

"Can you feed her while I go take a shower?" Terreka gave me our daughter.

I stared into her little eyes and regret hit me. Majesty was beautiful, but I thought about all the miscarriages Cori had and how I wasn't down to wait to see what the problem was with her. I placed the small bottle in my daughter's mouth as she started squirming in my arms. I remembered taking care of Kj when he was this size. Cori and I were pregnant at the time we had taken Kj in and the stress between Kenny and Paris had caused that miscarriage. We both moved on and kept trying, but every time we conceived, she miscarried.

I finished feeding my daughter, burped her and laid her back down in her bed that was nestled in the corner of Terreka's room. She was too afraid to let her sleep in her own room, so I had put the bed in here. I laid back on the bed and contemplated

94

calling Cori back to make sure she was all right, but the shower turned off. I put my phone back on the dresser and waited for Terreka to come out of the bathroom.

"What time did you get in last night?" she questioned.

"It was late. Majesty was up when I walked in, so I spent some time with her before I showered and crawled into the bed with you."

"Where did you go?"

"I went out."

"Were you with her?"

"No," I lied.

"I know you're lying, but I don't have a way to prove it. Mari, I'm not going to play second and I've told you that. You made your bed, now lay in it," Terreka stated before leaving me in the bedroom.

I was so ready to get back to work. I had taken off to help her around the house with the baby but the days weren't going by fast enough. I left my game at the house with Cori so Kj could have something to do, but that was my calming mechanism. Being shut in with Terreka was going to be a challenge. Terreka wouldn't be able to handle the truth if I told her half of the things I did to my wife last night. I leaned back on the bed with my phone in my hand. I hit Cori's name to send her a text.

Me: I'm sorry.

Cori: Please leave me alone.

Me: I messed up. Just promise me you'll forgive me.

She never responded.

Me: Please Cori.

My phone was snatched out of my hand. I didn't even try to fight Terreka for my phone back. I was caught red-handed.

"So, you begging her now?"

"I just want her to forgive me. She's still my wife, Terreka. I cheated on my wife!" I yelled, scaring her and waking up Majesty.

"You better get your mind right and decide where you want to be," Terreka spat.

"I'm here, ain't I?" I looked at her.

"Physically, you are, but I don't feel like you're here emotionally."

"Give me time. I can't stop loving my wife. There's history there and it takes time for that love to fade. Now, if you got a problem with me at least checking to make sure she straight, then you need to check yourself as a woman."

Terreka rolled her eyes at me as she walked out the room with the baby. I had to keep it real with her. There was no need in hiding the fact that my love for Cori was going to take a while to go away. I talked a lot of trash to her the night I left, but it was only to pump myself up.

♥

I had just dropped Terreka and Majesty off at home. Majesty had her checkup and I was heading to work. I was so glad to finally be getting out of the house. I needed to stop and get gas and grab something to eat for lunch because I was going to be working late. I was going to work a double just to make a little extra change. It had been three weeks since I had seen or talked to Cori and I was starting to worry about her and planned to stop by tomorrow before work.

I pulled up to the gas station that was connected to a Subway. I planned on knocking two birds out with one stone. After I had pumped the gas, I walked into Subway. I ordered my food and while my sandwich was being toasted, I fixed my drink. The sound of Cori's voice made me overfill my cup, causing it to spill all over the floor.

"Hey, Mari."

She looked really cute in a floral, off the shoulder dress. She had a new tattoo on her shoulder that said *Freedom.* Her hair was in braids and I could see the youthfulness in her face. Her skin was clear and the sting of losing her was evident on my face.

"How are you?" I asked.

"You ready to order your usual?" a dude asked her.

"Yea, give me a minute," Cori replied.

"Who is that?" I asked.

"That's Syeer, my co-worker."

"Tell him when you talking to me, don't interrupt. That's rude."

"Mari, don't do that. He doesn't even know who you are," Cori explained.

"Why is that?"

"I'm not about to stand here and do this with you," Cori scoffed.

She tried to walk away from me, but I grabbed her by her elbow.

"Let me go, Mari."

"Aye, she said let her go."

"Stay out of my business. Go over there with your suit on and order my wife her sandwich before we have a problem," I spat.

"You a funny cat. Don't let my suit fool you, patna."

"Man, go 'head on. We both know you ain't from the streets," I told him.

"Try me and we'll see who really from the streets," he stated.

"Syeer, give me a minute," Cori said.

We eyed each other down before he walked off to grab
their food.

"So, that's you?" I asked.

"You really don't have any room to talk, but to answer your
question, no, we're not dating. He's my co-worker and a friend,"
she explained.

"That's how you dress at work?"

"The office is actually closed today. We had a faulty fire
alarm and Syeer and I have work to do, so we met up for lunch.
It's no big deal."

"No big deal? I'll stop by when I get off tonight and he
better not be there. How's Kj?"

"He's still with Paris, but he's doing good."

"A'ight, I better get out of here before I'm late."

I kissed Cori on her cheek before I got my stuff and walked
out. I felt like a sucker watching my wife laughing in another
dude's face. I started my car and left, heading to work. We
hadn't been split long, but I was starting to regret my decision.
Cori hadn't looked that good in so long. I didn't take into
account her feelings as her husband. I just wanted her to stay in
the house and take care of Kj and me. Evidently, I had missed
all the signs.

I ended up leaving work early because I felt sick. I wasn't
physically sick, but I was emotionally sick. I knew the look that

Syeer dude had in his eyes. He wanted my wife and she was too naïve to see it. I wasn't going to give her up that easily. I headed to Terreka's to shower and check on them before I headed to my real home.

"Hey, baby," Terreka greeted me.

"Wassup?" I rushed to the bathroom.

"What you doing off so early?" she asked from behind the shower curtain.

I ran my head up under the water, rinsing the shampoo out of my hair. I could feel the cool air from Terreka pulling the curtain back.

"Did you hear me?"

"Yes, I heard you, Terreka. I'm off because I don't feel well. Is that okay?" I eyed her.

"I was just making sure everything was okay. No need for the attitude."

I finished washing myself and ignored her as she fumbled around in the bathroom. She was never this way when she was number two, but now she was the main woman and she was insecure. When I went to the bathroom, to the porch, or moved around the house, she was right there on me. It was really aggravating, and I had asked her to stop, but she still didn't get it. I turned the shower off and got out, wrapping my towel around my lower body as I went into the closet to grab something to put on.

"You about to leave? I thought maybe we could spend some time together with Majesty," Terreka said sadly.

"I'll be back later. I got something I need to do really quick," I told her without looking at her.

I went into Majesty's room and placed a kiss on her fat cheek before I walked out the door. I headed straight to my house, hoping Cori was home. I kind of wanted to see Kj, too, but Paris was hogging him, for some odd reason. I wasn't going to Paris' house because we could never see eye to eye when it came to Kj.

I was glad to see Cori's car in the driveway. I hit the doorbell and looked around to make sure none of my neighbors were out staring. I was the man of this house and it felt weird to not have a key. I could hear Cori's slides hitting the wooden floors as she walked towards the door. The door popped open and she looked up at me before she walked off, leaving me at the door. Her braids were now in a French braid and she was wearing a pair of shorts and one of my old wife beaters. Even with Kj not here, she was still cooking and kept the house clean. My stomach started to growl as I followed her to the kitchen.

"It smells good in here," I told her.

"Are you hungry?"

"I mean, I can eat a little something."

"Your girl ain't on her job, but I guess I'll feed you and send you on about your way," Cori said with an attitude. "That's the least your *wife* can do."

"Why you got to do all that?"

"The same reason you did what you did earlier. It doesn't feel good to see me happy, does it? I'm not even kicking it with dude like that. He's becoming a really good friend and listener."

I bit down on the inside of my jaw, trying to make sure I said the right words as it pertained to Cori.

"Bruh want you, trust me. I know the look he has in his eyes. I look at you the same way."

"Syeer does not want me. I'm not his type. I've seen his type of woman, and I ain't it." She giggled.

"What's so funny? You act like you want him to want you."

"Jealous?" Cori asked.

"I have nothing to be jealous about. You still belong to me until we get a divorce and I don't see that happening no time soon."

"You don't come in here and dictate anything. You lost that privilege when you walked out on this marriage. Now, eat your food and go home to the woman you fell in love with." Cori slammed my food down in front of me and walked off.

I looked at the plate and my mouth watered. She had cooked homemade mash potatoes, roast with carrots and celery and cabbage. I had to fight with my stomach, but I needed to go and talk to her before I could enjoy my food. She was in my man cave with the game controller in her hand and she didn't even acknowledge me as I walked into the room. I picked up the other controller and joined in as she played *Call of Duty*.

I left my phone in the car intentionally so I could give Cori all my attention. Terreka was probably blowing my phone up because it was close to eleven at night and I had just got Cori to at least laugh and talk to me. We both had work in the morning, but I didn't want to leave her. I slid next to her and placed a kiss on her lips. When she didn't stop me, I kissed her a little more passionately the second time. I dropped my controller and grabbed her around her waist until her body was under mine. She was a lot smaller than me, so it didn't take much force to move her until we were both comfortable on the sofa. I knew my wife loved me because of the way she looked me in my eyes before I started kissing her again.

Our kissing turned into something else and we were now lying naked on the floor. Cori wouldn't look at me. I could tell she regretted what we had just done, but I didn't feel bad, she was my wife. Terreka was the mother of my child, but I was second guessing if I even had feelings for her at this point. Cori had a tight hold on my heart and I couldn't leave her alone.

"I love you, Cori." I broke the silence between us.

"Don't tell me that, Mari. Go ahead and leave while I'm still up. No need to sneak out and go home," she said, rising from the floor, putting her clothes back on.

"I'm not going anywhere. Let's go shower and get in our bed," I clarified.

After another round with Cori in the shower, we were now lying in bed with her head on my chest while I played in her braids. It was like we were back to us. This was what I wanted the whole time. It was all my fault, really, and I had no problem telling her that.

"I really like this. It feels like we're young again. I messed up big time," I told her.

"Mari, you don't give things time. Marriages go through seasons. We were in our winter months, and everything dies in the winter or hibernates. Spring and summer are the most joyous times in a marriage, but if you're going to run when winter comes, then we won't work."

"Winter only lasts a few months, and what we were going through was going on for a little longer."

"I'm not talking about the physical season, Mari. Our winter could last a year or two; it's all about working through it. I'm too tired to get into it right now. I got work in the morning."

"I need you to stop hanging out with that Syeer dude."

"I can't stop hanging out with him. We work together and sometimes have to work late. We work on multi-million-dollar deals. If it wasn't for him, I wouldn't be able to do my job. The answer is no."

"If it's work related, cool, but all that other stuff is out the window."

"Are you asking me or telling me? I'm not your woman, Mari, did you forget? I know after tonight I won't see you again for another month. I get that, but I refuse to give my body up to another man who's not my husband."

I took in everything she was saying and planned on making it a point not to make it a whole month. By the time I got back to Terreka, she was going to put a tracking device on me. I wrapped my arms around my wife and went to sleep.

Terreka

I had just laid Majesty back down for the fourth time tonight. It was now almost four in the morning and Mari still hadn't made it home. I had a feeling he was with his wife. I was a fool to think that he was just going to walk away from her because I had a baby. It was all good, though. I wasn't hard up for him. I did love him, but I could easily find another man just like I had found him. I climbed into my bed and went to sleep peacefully.

My eyes popped open as Mari came tiptoeing into our bedroom. I peeped at the clock and it was now six in the morning. He stripped down and went to the bathroom to take a shower. I waited until he was in the shower before I jumped out of bed to get his phone. I put in Majesty's birthday and his phone came to life. I thumbed through until I reached his wife's number. I bit down on my bottom lip as I peeked into the bathroom when I hit the call button.

"Did you forget something?" his wife spoke into the phone.

For a minute, I just sat there, but I realized I needed to say what I had called for before Mari got out of the shower. I swallowed the dry lump in my throat before I spoke.

"Yea, he left something."

"Excuse me?"

"I want you to hear me clearly when I say this. Mari is with his daughter and me now. He left your rotten vagina. You'll never be able to give him what I gave him. Last night was your last night with my man. I'm glad I don't know who you are, or I would handle you personally. I hope you enjoyed yourself, but Mari belongs to me. Go ahead and draw up the divorce papers because he's not coming back," I said before the phone was slapped out of my hand.

"What the hell are you doing? Are you talking to my wife?" he angrily asked.

He bent over to pick his phone up, but she had hung up. He tried calling her back, but she wouldn't answer. I watched him try to call her back at least three times before I couldn't take it anymore. I charged at him and started swinging on him. My blows were nothing to him because he pushed me off him, causing me to fall on my butt.

"It just wasn't good enough that I left my wife for you, huh? You had to go and call her and be messy? She didn't deserve that, Terreka. You knew I was married when you started dealing with me. I'm not about to stop talking to her because you're insecure. What you so insecure about, huh? You worried, ain't you? Your side chick spot open and now you scared. Let me get dressed for work before I hurt you." He grabbed his clothes and got dressed in the guest room.

It took him about five minutes to get dressed before I heard the front door slam. Majesty started screaming at the top of her lungs. I had a checkup today and I wanted Mari to go with me so he could watch Majesty, but the way everything had gone was not what I had planned when I called his wife. I took Majesty back in the room with me and rocked her back to sleep. I had to find a ride to the doctor because my car was in the shop.

Once I woke up, I called the only other person I knew to call for a ride. We hadn't talked in ages, but I needed someone and I was willing to pay.

"Hey, I hate to bother you, but I was wondering could you give my baby and me a ride to the doctor?"

"How long has it been?"

"It's been a long time. Look, I need you this one time and I promise you'll never hear from me again."

"You still in the same spot? It's been almost three years since I've seen you."

"Yes, same spot."

I hung up the phone and got myself dressed before I wiped Majesty down and got her dressed as well. My nerves were all over the place and I hoped I was doing the right thing by calling him to come get me. I started a load of laundry and straightened the kitchen just to pass the time.

It was close to Mari's lunch break and I didn't want him calling while I was around this man. I waited on the porch for him once he texted and told me he was about five minutes away. An all-black Benz pulled up to the curb and rolled the window down slightly, signifying that it was him. That was something we used to do when I was younger. I grabbed Majesty's car seat and quickly walked towards the car, climbing into the backseat like back in the day.

"You look good," he said.

"Thank you. Nice car."

"Courtesy of the wife. How's it been going?"

"It's been going good. My car is in the shop, so until they can figure out what's wrong with it, I'll be stranded in the house," I explained to him.

"You don't have to explain your situation to me. Which doctor's office you going to?"

"It's downtown by the big Bank of America building."

As he drove I played with Majesty to trying to keep my focus off of him. In the back of my mind I was wishing Majesty was his. I wouldn't have a care in the world if she was. He was always good to me and I'm sure he would be a great father.

"Do you need me to wait for you?" he asked as we pulled up to the complex where the doctor's office was located.

"If you have the time."

"Wife is away with her sisters on their annual girls' trip, so I got a little time. I'll wait out here."

I climbed out, grabbing my daughter and her belongings. Things between us were so weird. He was always a gentleman, but all I could think about was Mari. I knew he had a lot of questions. The last time we talked, it ended on a bad note. I'd had a baby since then and I could tell from the look on his face that he was confused when I was carrying a newborn baby.

My doctor's appointment went well and I was released to go back to work. I hadn't worked since I had gotten pregnant with my daughter. I only had a high school diploma and no desire to go back to school. At twenty-four, I had a three-bedroom apartment and a used car. I was able to maintain my rent for the apartment because of Mari. I only worked in fast food and he made sure after I quit, my rent was paid for a year. If he left, then I would have to get a job. I wasn't about to lose him, though. And I for sure wasn't about to be number two in his life again. I got back in the car with my daughter screaming because she was hungry.

"Could you hold her while I make her a bottle real quick?" I handed her over.

"What am I supposed to do with it?" He frowned.

"It's not an it. It's a girl, and her name is Majesty," I stated as I made her bottle.

He gave her back to me in the backseat. Placing the bottle in her mouth, she instantly ceased her crying. I looked up at him staring at me in the rearview mirror.

"You going back home?"

"Yes, please."

He pulled off, heading towards my house.

"So, the fella you got this baby from, is he in her life?"

"Yes, he's actually at work right now."

"So, you telling me he didn't want to go to the doctor with you? I thought I taught you better than that."

"Don't do that. You didn't teach me anything. This was the reason I had to leave you alone: you always thought you ruled me."

"No, you stopped dealing with me because my wife threatened you."

I rolled my eyes at him. He was right, though. My thoughts ran off to the day his wife showed up on my doorstep.

I was gathering my things to go on a business trip with Adrian. We did this often. I was able to see the world and be with the man I loved. I placed my passport in my purse before I forcefully zipped up the suitcase. I always over packed and

Adrian had to pay more for my luggage to make it on the plane. I dragged the suitcase up to the living room and waited for him to pull up. I grabbed a Lunchable out the refrigerator as the doorbell chimed. I opened the door to the most beautiful dark-skinned woman. Her hair flowed in the wind and the golden undertone of her skin was reflected by the sun.

"May I help you?" I asked.

"Are you Terreka?"

"Yes, that's me." I looked at her suspiciously.

"Can I come in?"

"I'm not sure. What is this about?"

"I'm not going to harm you. Trust me, if I wanted to, I would've done it a long time ago."

I stepped aside to let her in and she let out a loud sigh as she looked at my luggage.

"Going on a trip?" she asked.

"Yes, I'm about to head to China."

"With Adrian?" she quizzed.

"Excuse me?"

"With my husband, Adrian? Is that who you're going with?"

"I...I had no idea," I explained.

"Oh, it's fine, sweetie. I'm sure he didn't tell you he was married with three daughters. But, now that you know, I need

you to unpack your bags and never contact my husband again. You don't have to worry about him bothering you either. Are we understood?" She pierced me with her hazel eyes.

"Yea...yea, I got it," I stuttered.

She walked out the door, but not before slapping me across my face.

"You young girls are so dumb. If a man never stays with you overnight but only takes you on business trips and spends money freely, he's married. But I guess you're too young to even see the signs. I hate to have to come back."

She walked off, getting into a shiny red BMW. It was then, at the age of twenty-one, I became cold-hearted about men.

By the time I snapped out of my daydream, he was pulling up in front of my house.

"I'm assuming you're still afraid of my wife?"

"I'm not afraid of anyone, but I don't like playing number two."

"Did I ever treat you like number two?"

"Yea, you did."

"My money didn't, though. I made sure you were good and that little beat up car you drove was about to be replaced until my wife found out. I can still get you that car if you want it. It's just between us; your man doesn't even have to know. You fresh out the doctor"

"I don't think we should be having this conversation. Thank you for giving me and my daughter a ride."

"Hit me up if you change your mind." He winked.

Adrian met me while I was in my senior year in high school. He did something called telehealth at the school. I got sick and ended up in the nurse's office where he was setting up everything and training them on how to use the software. The attraction was instant. He couldn't focus because he was so busy looking at me. After taking a Tylenol, I left out and he caught up with me. He got my number and we linked up that weekend. At the time, he was twenty-seven and I had just turned eighteen.

We spent so much time together. He told me not to tell anyone about him because of the big age gap between us. I graduated and moved out of my mama's house and into my apartment. Adrian paid the rent, but I worked at McDonald's so my mama wouldn't question me. When I turned twenty, I stopped working to travel with Adrian. I was living the life with him. I still had feelings for him and I could only imagine what my life would be like if I had never stopped sleeping with him. I sat on my sofa, rocking Majesty, just thinking about what Adrian had said. Mari was still spending time with his wife, so there was nothing wrong with me having a little fun too.

Paris

"So, you leave and pop back up pregnant?" Kenny asked.

He was so close that I could smell what he had eaten for breakfast. He was always checking me about my business but never wanted to be with me. I pushed him from in front of me and went to my living room. The reason he was here was for Kj, not me.

"Are you here to finally tell your son he has a father, or to bash me?"

"I'm here for my son; definitely not your rat behind. I hate that I even laid down with you and gave you the opportunity to have my child. Who leaves their child to go run off with another man anyway, Paris? Oh, I forgot. You do. I should slap the fire from you, but you looking kind of good in them tights, so I'll let you slide."

I laughed because Kenny was clearly in his feelings because I was carrying another man's baby. The only reason I was still hanging on to this pregnancy was because Novi was paid, and I was holding one of his biggest secrets. It was strange that he hadn't called to check up on me or anything, but my

115

deposits still hit the account faithfully. I noticed a little extra a few times too.

"Well, let me go get him so you can break it down to him that his father has been absent for seven years. Oh, what a joy this is about to be." I tried walking off, but not before Kenny grabbed my arm.

"Wait, are you sure he's ready for this? I mean, I know I haven't been the best father physically, but I always made sure he got what he needed."

"He's ready because he always asks Cori and me about you. Once he looks at you, it's like looking at himself. If you're afraid, then let me know before I get his feelings involved. I don't want him meeting you and then your wife finds out and then you vanish out of my son's life," I explained.

"I wouldn't do that. I want to be in his life, I just don't want to be with you."

"I'm cool with that, Kenny. Just know when your wife is getting on your nerves, don't call me." I walked off in the direction of my son's room.

"Kj, I have someone here who wants to meet you."

He never took his eyes off his game. He was biting down on his bottom lip just like Kenny did when he was in deep thought.

"Come on, and I promise to take you to see Auntie Cori afterward."

Kj threw the controller down and ran out the room. By the time I made it to the living room, Kj was standing there, staring at his twin.

"It's okay, Kj, I'm your father."

Kj looked up at me for confirmation and I shook my head and grabbed his hand to walk with him over to Kenny. Kenny held his hand out for Kj to come to him and he slowly walked up to him. It made my heart smile to see the two of them together. No one could tell me that Kenny didn't get me pregnant on purpose. It was his way of controlling me and what I did with my body, which was why he was so upset to see me with a stomach.

While they bonded, I went into the kitchen to finish cooking. I wasn't the best at it, but Cori did teach me a few things. I knew how to fry chicken and cook a good pot of rice. I was still learning the whole cornbread thing, but I knew how to throw some Hawaiian rolls in the oven and a can of vegetables on the stove. It was just Kj and me, so I didn't have to please anyone else.

"I'm heading out. I'll be back tomorrow to pick him up and take him to get a few things." Kenny walked into the kitchen.

"Okay," I responded.

"I appreciate you for giving me a son."

"Hey, that's all I was good for, you know?"

"It's not like that, Paris. I thought you were going to be the one until I met my wife."

"Thanks for reminding me. You can see yourself out now."

"I'll text you." He kissed my cheek.

My heart stung. Hearing that come out of his mouth was painful. Now that he had gotten that off his chest, I wanted to know what kept him coming back even while he was married. There was something Kenny wasn't telling me and I was going to get it out of him one way or another. Kj and I ate and all he could talk about was his father and how excited he was that his daddy was coming to get him and take him shopping. Kj was no stranger to a male figure in his life because Mari was very present in his life.

"We still going to see Auntie Cori? I got to tell her about my daddy."

"Yes, let me clean up and we will head over there."

Kj ran off and I already knew he was going back to his game. I cleaned the kitchen and went to change into something more comfortable before Kj and I got in the car and headed to Cori's. She would call and check on Kj but she never came over. I should've been a better friend, but I was afraid to leave my house in fear of Novi lurking somewhere. I looked over my contract so many times but could never find any loopholes. Novi had it written up just right. Now it was all about having this baby and moving on. I pulled up behind Cori's car, paying close attention to the car that was parked on the curb. I let Kj ring the doorbell.

Cori answered the door in a pair of jogging pants and one of Mari's old shirts. Her hair was braided so pretty. Something was different about her and I didn't know what it was because I was so disconnected.

"Hey, Kj." Cori grabbed him and placed kisses all over his face. "I missed you so much. Uncle Mari bought you some new games and you haven't been here to play them."

"Well, hey to you, too, friend. Can we come in?" I asked with an attitude.

"You know you don't have to ask that question. The last time we talked, you ended up kicking me out your house and slamming the door in my face. I'm not like that, though. As long as you're Kj's mother, I'll always have a relationship with you. I was just so excited to see my nephew. I miss his presence in my house. I just got in the habit of not cooking a lot of food since it's just me."

"My bad for that. Blame it on my pregnancy hormones."

"Girl, get in here." Cori pulled me in for a hug. I couldn't help but notice the fine man sitting at the table.

"Who is that?" I whispered with my face screwed up.

I mean, Mari cheated, but I didn't want another man around my son but Mari.

"That's my co-worker, Syeer. Come on so I can introduce you."

I hesitated because I felt that at any moment, Mari was going to walk through the door and bust all of us across the head.

"Girl, come on."

There was no way Cori was spending so much time with this man and wasn't turned on. He was turning me on just standing here staring at him. He was sexy, tall and had just the right amount of hair on his face. He looked like a good kisser from the looks of his juicy, pink lips. He licked his lips as he looked up from his computer. For a second, I wished I wasn't pregnant because I would definitely have a one-night stand with this brother. He was just that fine. Whew, let me get myself together.

"You can stop drooling now, Paris."

"Girl, don't embarrass me like that," I told Cori. "Hi, I'm Cori's best friend, Paris, and this is my son, Kj."

"I'm Syeer, Cori's co-worker. I've heard so much about both of you guys. Cori really has love for you two."

"I hope everything was good." I side-eyed Cori.

"Of course, it was good," Cori interrupted.

"Well, I think we got a good start on the project. I'll call you tonight to touch bases with you before we have a meeting tomorrow. Don't stress, we got this." He placed a kiss on her cheek before he packed up his laptop and left.

"What the hell, Cori? I know you sleeping with that tall glass of chocolate milk."

"Nope," she responded before flopping on the sofa.

"Girl, I know you lying. Tell me all about it." I patted her on her leg as I sat down next to her.

"I'm serious, Paris. I am not sleeping with him. We don't see each other like that. He's like a big brother to me."

"So, he's up for grabs?"

"Don't you dare stick your claws in that man. He knows you're pregnant."

"Ugh, you talk too much, Cori."

"Girl, please. You need to focus on yourself and learning how to be by yourself if you ain't going to be with Novi."

"Girl, ain't nobody worried about him. Everything we had was fake. All I need him to do is make sure he keeps making deposits into my account. He doesn't even have to have anything to do with this baby," I told Cori.

"You at least need to give him updates."

"Enough about me. What's going on with you and Mari? I haven't been there for you like I should have. It was corny of me."

"On a serious note, I'm not worried about Mari. Do I love him? Yes, I do, but I can't deal with the drama his baby mama's trying to start. If anything, I should be the one starting drama with her because I'm the wife. Do you know she called me from his phone telling me to leave him alone? I don't know what happened because I hung up. He tried calling me back, but I haven't answered. I don't have time to play with Mari. If this continues, I'm going to have to get a divorce."

"You wait until I drop this baby. I'll find out who she is and drag her for you. You know you're not much of a fighter, but me, baby? Oohhh, she just wait. Does he post any pictures of her?" I asked.

"No, only pictures of him and the baby. She's so gorgeous."

"Well, she doesn't mean nothing to him. He'll be back."

"What am I supposed to do? Just wait for my husband to get tired of playing house?"

"Chile, Mari loves the ground you walk on. Y'all got the issue with having a baby, but other than that, y'all good. He's just happy about the baby. Once that wears off, he'll be

122

crawling back, and then you'll be dealing with baby mama from hell."

"See, that's what I'm not ready to deal with."

"Don't worry, every time she says something out the way, just call me. She'll get tired of me putting my hands on her after a while."

Cori and I kicked it for hours until Kj fell asleep waiting for us to finish talking. I saw how many times Mari called her and she ignored every one of his calls. I was shocked he hadn't popped up yet. Cori took down a whole bottle of wine by herself just telling me about her problems with Mari. I had to find out who his baby mama was. There was no way she was about to ruin my best friend's marriage. The side chick was not about to win. I laughed on the inside because I was a side chick and I never won.

"I'm about to head out. I know you got work in the morning and you're going to need some strong black coffee if you don't get some sleep now." I laughed.

"I really missed you. I'm so glad we're back on track."

"Me too."

I kissed her cheek and opened the door with Kj sleeping in my arms.

"Why you got him in your arms and you pregnant?" Mari asked as soon as we opened the door.

"You know us single girls have to make things happen on our own," I said in my petty voice.

"Hand me my nephew and I'll walk him to the car."

Mari took him out of my arms and proceeded to the car.

"I knew he was going to pop up. Be nice to him," I said through my teeth to Cori.

"To hell with him." She rolled her eyes and went back in the house, making sure to lock the door.

"Your girl tripping," Mari expressed.

"Nah, she ain't tripping, she's hurt. If you want her, you know you can't be playing house with that other chick. Cori has been too good to all of us. She doesn't have a bad bone in her body. She loves you so much that she may wait for you to get your head on straight. For the sake of my friend, I hope you wake up and see what you got in front of you. By the way, tell your baby muva she got to see me when I have this baby for calling Cori and starting drama."

"I handled that already."

"Nah, you didn't hear me. I said she got to see me. I don't care about what you did or said." I got in my car and drove off as Mari beat on the door.

Cori

"**B**aby, please open the door. I just want to talk to you. I want to let you know I had no idea she got hold of my phone," Mari whined from the outside of my door.

I listened as he begged with hot tears streaming down my face. I hated that I loved him so much. I wanted to open the door, but the hurt I felt wouldn't let me. I only felt good when I was around someone. If I was by myself, all I did was cry until I was sick. I thought I was getting somewhere when I changed my look, but every time Mari's name popped up on my phone or I ran into him, those feelings rushed back. I hated it.

"Please, Cori. I'll sit out here all night if I have to. I'll pop up at your job if I have to. I suggest you open the door."

"Get away from my door, Mari."

"Like I said, I ain't going nowhere."

"Go home to your baby and leave me alone. Don't come back to me until you're ready to come back for good." I wiped my tears and shut the porch light off.

I tossed and turned. I even got up to see if Mari was still out there and he was. He would walk from his car to the front porch. Around four, I heard his car start and him pulling off. Tomorrow I had a very important meeting and this was not what

I needed. I had about three hours to sleep before I had to be back up. I forced my eyes closed, but sleep just wouldn't come. Throwing the cover off, I got up and made some tea and stayed up until it was time for work. At least, I thought I was.

"Cori, are you all right? The meeting starts in thirty minutes and you aren't here. I mean, I can handle the majority of it on my own, but I do need you for some of the information." Syeer's voice boomed through the speaker in my car.

"I'm in traffic. I promise I'll be there. I overslept; it was a long night."

"I'll stall for as long as I can, just get here as fast as you can," he said before ending the call.

I hit the steering wheel repeatedly.

"Okay, calm down, Cori. You got this. You got this. Don't let anything stress you out right now," I told myself.

I pressed down on my horn, praying that whatever was going on that was slowing traffic down would miraculously disappear. As long as I had stayed in this city, I had never seen it this congested. I placed in an alternate route in my GPS. It would add on ten minutes, but I could possibly cut it down if I went a little over the speed limit. I turned off the exit and took the back way to my job. I cut the ten extra minutes, but I was still late for the meeting. I ran to the elevators with my glasses sliding off my sweaty face.

"There she is," Syeer nervously said.

"I'm so sorry I'm late. Traffic was backed up, so I had to take an alternate route."

I unpacked all my stuff and noticed I had left the most important thing: my USB port. Panic had set in as I looked around the room full of multi-millionaires and I was fumbling. Syeer placed his hands on mine to settle me. He pulled a USB out of his inside pocket and placed it in the computer. He had literally saved my life. I smiled at him and he nodded at me signaling me to do what I did best. No one knew the way to a woman's heart like a woman. The company was trying to target women to buy their perfume. I worked the room like I hadn't been thirty minutes late. By the time I was done, the owner was smiling, and so was my boss.

"You did great," Syeer whispered in my ear.

"We did great. I couldn't have done it without you. I owe you big time."

"How about a dinner date? My parents are having this big dinner at their house and I kind of need a date."

"I owe you that much."

"Okay, it's this weekend. Be ready by six and I'll swing by and get you."

"I'll be ready. Anything I need to know about your parents before I pop up?" I asked.

"They will love you. Be yourself."

I was now in my office, trying to catch my breath. It had been an eventful morning and I couldn't take anything else happening at this moment.

"I figured I would be able to find you up in here. This is a nice spot." Mari burst into my office.

"Please don't do this now, Mari," I begged.

"I'm not about to do anything to jeopardize your job. I've done enough bad in your life. I just wanted to see you, and since you denied me that last night, I decided to pop up. Your little co-worker wasn't too happy to see me."

"Don't be petty, Mari. What is it you want?"

"I wanted to apologize about Terreka calling you."

"Save your apologies, Mari. That's all you've been doing the past month and a half. I'm tired of hearing it. For you not to want me, you're constantly trying to talk to me. Are you ready to come home, or you trying to have both of us?" I eyed him from behind my desk.

"I'm saying I miss you."

"I don't need you to only pop up when you miss me, or you want to have sex with me. We've had more sex than we've had in months. How do you think I feel when you have sex with me and then go home to her? How do you think that makes me feel? You know what, you don't care, and I'm not about to waste my time trying to get you to understand how I feel. I just had the most stressful morning and I'm sitting here waiting to see if my meeting went well. You can leave." I dismissed him.

A tap on my door caught our attention.

"Hey, just wanted to let you know you hit a home run with the meeting today. He's signing the deal as we speak. Let's celebrate tonight; it's on me." Syeer winked.

"You ain't going," Mari said once Syeer was gone.

"I bet you I will. Now, you can go. I got work to do and you're distracting me." I waved him off.

I was glad I had changed banks so Mari wouldn't know how much this deal was going to bring me. I really changed it because once I went through the bank statements, I noticed he was slipping money out and swiping the card for hotel rooms. It was his money at the time, but I'll be dang if I let him use my hard-earned money to take care of his family. There was nothing Mari could tell me at this point. I was going out with my co-workers to celebrate. It was time for me to live since that was what he had been doing all this time.

I mostly stayed to myself, but I was finally hanging out with my office crew. If I wasn't with Syeer, I didn't hang out. Everyone was vibing and enjoying each other. Drinks were flowing and nobody was talking about work. This was something I could get used to. I went from depending on Mari to making a salary that would put him to shame. That still didn't stop me from loving him.

"Stop sitting here nursing that same glass of wine. Come dance with me," Syeer said.

"I am not about to dance in front of all these people I don't really know."

"Come on." He pulled my hand.

French Montana's song was playing, so I got into the groove of the music. I made sure not to push up on Syeer because I didn't want to give him any ideas. The Caribbean vibe was just what the doctor called for as I turned around, letting my small hips control my body. Syeer stepped back so he could check me out. What people didn't know about me was Paris and I would party all night in our younger days. I wasn't new to the whole partying thing, but it took me getting drunk, high off a date rape drug and getting raped to slow down and to this day I feel that was the reason I couldn't have kids. That turned me into the shy, quiet woman I was today. I figured that if I stayed to myself, no one would be able to violate me ever again. The only person that knew was Paris. She had actually found out who one of the boys was and did a little damage to his face with her famous baseball bat. I swear once Paris got loose, there was no stopping her.

Syeer grabbed my hips and danced along with me, making sure to keep space between us. We had danced through three songs before we were both winded and thirsty. I looked at my Apple watch and rolled my eyes. Mari had texted and told me he had been by the house and I wasn't there. I knew it was time for me to go. I didn't need Mari flipping out because it was late and I was out. I didn't want to give him any reason to think I was stepping out on our marriage like he was doing.

"I'm heading out, everyone."

Everyone said goodbye to me as Syeer and I walked out. He was such a gentleman for walking me to my car. I could feel my phone buzzing in my purse, but I ignored it because it was no one but Mari.

"I look forward to this weekend. Get home safe," he said before shutting my door.

I drove home in silence. The thought of ending my marriage came to the front of my mind. I was so thankful that Paris wasn't one of those friends who was like, 'if it was me, I would leave.' She spoke her piece and left it alone. No one knew how it felt to be in a marriage, and because someone messed up, you end everything. To you, I may have been a fool, but I did want to fight a little longer. Other than this incident, I had never known Mari to do anything outside of our marriage.

When I pulled up, Mari was parked in his normal spot. He hopped out before I could get my car in park and he didn't have an expression on his face. I grabbed my purse and shoes.

"This what married women do? Hang out all night?"

"Go home, Mari. I'm not in the mood to argue. I just want to get in my bed and go to sleep."

"I didn't come to argue. I just want to know why the sudden change in you."

I spun around and looked at him dead in his eyes. I wasn't the one who had changed and he was about to get the real scoop.

"Wait, did you just ask me why I changed? I didn't change, Mari, you did. This person you see right here is a person who had the love of her life walk out on her for another woman. What did you expect? Let me guess, you wanted me to sit around and cry over you and beg you to come back where you belong. Well, I've done my crying and begging and I'm not begging a man to do what he vowed to do. Just like you walked out on me over a month ago, I'm walking away from you tonight and I don't want to see you again unless you're coming home."

I walked off, leaving Mari standing in the driveway, dumbfounded. His feelings were hurt, but so were mine. I had lied when I said I was done crying because as soon as I shut the door, the dam broke and the tears flowed freely down my face. He would never get the benefit of seeing me cry ever again.

Novi

I had tried to be nice and polite about the situation between Paris and me, but she was still my wife and she was still carrying my child, which she refused to give me an update on. She did manage to send me a picture, letting me know it was a little girl, but that was all I knew. I put extra money in her account just to keep her quiet about my secrets. I didn't expect my boyfriend to come back from his trip so soon. Most times, he would be gone for up to six months. I felt that would be plenty of time to get Paris in her own house and they would never know about each other. I closed my suitcase and grabbed my wallet off my dresser. Before I could make it to the door, the nagging started.

"I see you leaving again without telling me. You going to chase that girl down?"

"I've asked you to stay out of my business as it pertains to her. As long as she's carrying my child, you cannot, and I do mean cannot, say a word to me about her," I expressed.

"Oh, okay. Go ahead then. We'll see how far you'll get when I shut all those credit cards down. Oh, and that money you keep sending her, I'm about to put a stop to that too."

"Are you making empty threats, Moody?" I got in his face.

"Nothing empty here but this big house since you've been chasing her. You thought I didn't know you flew to the US just to see if you could keep tabs on her. I know everything you do, Novi. That's why I made you the way you are." He rubbed my chest.

"Get your hands off me. You didn't make me. I found you behind a dumpster with your butt bust open. I made you. Now, run along and go make me some money like you usually do with your million-dollar business partners who are just as undercover as I am. If you want to spill secrets, then let's do it. Now, I'm about to go and talk with her so we can come to some common ground. If you got a problem with that, then be gone when I come back." I grabbed my suitcase and walked out the door.

Moody was Brazil's biggest prostitute. He had a thing for telling people we were together, but truthfully, we weren't. Just like Paris, we had an agreement. Since he liked to sleep with men and I liked money, I got rich from sending him away to make friends with some of the most prestigious people in the world. After he had swooned them, it was nothing for them to spend money and give him any amount he asked for. Moody was a very jealous person and because he tried several times to turn me out, it never worked. So, now here I was, sitting on a plane, flying to tell Paris the truth. A woman like her was very strong-willed and getting her to believe me was going to be hard. I still didn't know what Moody had said to her, but I was sure it wasn't good for her to run out.

I replayed that day over and over in my head, trying to see what had made her leave without calling me. Moody surely wasn't the only reason. Then again, women didn't like to be cheated on with another man. I had about four men and three women in my prostitution ring. It brought me a lot of money. Playing in the NBA was really what I wanted, but when that never happened, I moved across seas and saw how freely I could get away with it. My ultimate goal was to make Paris my main attraction. Getting her pregnant was my way of making her stay while I groomed and trained her.

I had been inside my mother's house for two days now. I was trying to get myself together before I dealt with Paris, but my anger was trying to get the best of me. I picked up a picture of my mother and I and thought about how good my life used to be. My mother was my source of strength. She went to all my games even while working two or three jobs at a time, trying to make sure I had everything I needed. She would be so happy to know she had a grandchild on the way. I placed the picture down and headed to get dressed so I could head to Paris'.

When I pulled up, there was a man outside playing with a little boy. I checked the address on the mailbox and on the house again to make sure I was at the right place. I put the car in park and climbed out. They ceased with throwing the ball and the little boy looked at me in amazement. The man, on the other hand, had envy in his eyes. Once I got a good look at him, I remembered him from school.

"Can I help you?"

"Paris here?"

"Yea, she in the house. Don't I know you?"

"Yea, we went to school together."

"Novi? Man, you were the man in school. What you want with Paris, though?"

"Oh, I'm still the man."

I left him outside and walked into the house. Paris was a very clean woman. It all made sense to me who this man was outside once I saw all the pictures of the little boy. Paris had lied about her son, and now I was wondering what else she had lied to me about. I know she didn't think she was going to let this dude raise my child.

"Hey, y'all ready to eat?" Paris turned around and all the color drained from her face.

"You surprised to see me? Don't be." I smiled at her. "I'll take a plate, too, since we will all be one big happy family soon. I didn't even know you had a son. When did you plan on telling me that?" I raised my eyebrow.

"Paris, is this who you pregnant by?"

"Kj, could you go to your room for me and I'll let you know when you can come out," she told her son.

"What's your name, my man?" I asked Paris' baby father. I went to school with him, but he was irrelevant to me, so I didn't know his name.

"It's Kenny."

"Oh, Kenny, see, you may have a son by her, but she's my wife. I don't know what you thought this was, but you're not needed at this time."

"Paris, you better get your boy. He don't know me well enough to be trying me like we back in high school or something. I'm not about to leave you here with my son, so we might as well sit down and eat dinner together, just like you said. Whatever you got to say to Paris, you can say in front of me." Kenny sat down in the chair.

I peeled off my coat and threw it on the back of my chair. I sat right across from him and waited for Paris to serve me. I wasn't concerned with him because if he was so important to Paris, surely, she wouldn't have stayed with me as long as she had. I knew her feelings for me were changing once she started checking me about staying out late at night. Since I had been married to her, I had never once cheated. I was out working. In her mind, she thought I was gay, but she was my decoy because

138

people were speculating. Paris was beautiful and it threw everyone off when she popped up on the scene.

We both watched as Paris nervously fixed the first plate. I was really trying to see who she was going to serve first. Paris was so terrified her hands were trembling. I didn't come for trouble, but if Kenny wanted to go there, we could go there. I never left home without being strapped. I had several guns stashed at my mother's house.

Paris walked up with two plates and sat my plate down, then Kenny's. That was the smartest move she could've ever done.

"So, you serve him before me? Don't forget who's been here for you the longest," Kenny spat.

"Calm down talking to my wife in that manner. I would hate for this to turn into something more serious." I eyed Kenny.

"What you trying to do?" Kenny rose as I placed some food into my mouth.

I chewed while he stood there looking like a fool. I took my gun from my waistband, placed it on the table and continued to eat. See, he knew the basketball player, but he knew nothing about the killer I really was. I would gladly introduce him to the real me.

"Novi, please put that away. My son is in the next room," Paris pleaded.

"Yea, about that. When did you plan on telling me? You can pack him up too because we're leaving tomorrow."

"My son ain't going nowhere."

"You sure?"

"Paris, you better talk to this dude. Send him back over to Cori's," Kenny stated.

"Why can't he go with you?" I asked. "Is it because your precious little wife doesn't know?"

"Don't speak on what you don't know," he said.

I leaned back in my chair. "Let's see what I know. Your apartment number is 1123, she drives a red Maxima, she works at a local doctor's office as a medical assistant and her parents live at—"

"That's enough!" Kenny yelled.

"Now that we have that established, Paris, we're leaving tomorrow."

"Can we talk about this? I mean, my son needs more time."

"Kenny, you can excuse yourself. Take your son with you for a few hours too."

"Kenny, please," Paris begged.

"I'll be back in an hour." Kenny got up from the table.

After they had left, it was just us at the table. Paris continued to eat as if I wasn't sitting here, staring at her.

"Okay, let's stop the games," she said, dropping her fork.

"Let's." I shrugged.

"Why are you here? We had an arrangement. You don't love me and I don't love you. I've been going to all my appointments and your baby is fine, so what else would you like to know?"

"Why did you leave?" I asked.

"Are you gay?" She watched me intensely to see if I would lie.

I looked her straight in her eyes. "No."

"Well, who was that guy who called himself confronting me?"

"You want the truth?"

She crossed her arms across her chest, resting them right on top of her stomach.

"You're not ready for the truth. You can't handle it."

"I tell you what I can handle: you shooting a woman in front of me, cold blooded."

I choked on my tea when she said that. For some reason, I had a feeling she was in my office that day.

"Don't speak on what you don't know," I told her.

"I know you were pissed about her doing a job. You killed her, so how do I know you're not going to kill me too? All you ever wanted was this baby. You don't want me, so after my time is up, then what?"

Paris was street smart. I wasn't going to be able to pull one over on her as easily as I thought. The more I stared at her, the more I thought about how beautiful she was. I could learn to love her. Who was I kidding? I could never love another woman.

"Are you ready to raise a girl?" I asked her.

"Novi, I can't go back to that house with you knowing that man is there. Do you know he tried to fight me? I can't just uproot my son from his school, his friends and family."

"You don't have to worry about Moody back home. I've straightened him out. As far as your son goes, if he doesn't come, then you have to find somewhere for him to go. My child will not be born here. I'll be back tomorrow to get you. Don't try to go running again because the next time I have to leave; it won't be nice."

Paris

"So, you just going to leave your son again? I swear I don't know what I was thinking by having a baby with you. I thought you were doing so much better. You know what, go ahead on with him. I'm not about to let Cori take care of my son for us. I'll take care of him. He needs me in his life. At least one of us loves him," Kenny ridiculed.

"Don't do that, Kenny," I sniffled.

"Paris, I swear you are dumb. I'll never forgive you if you leave."

"Kenny, just know I love my son. The bond we were forming was great. I don't want to leave him, but Brazil is not a place for him."

"Whatever, Paris." He waved me off.

I could not comprehend why he was so mad, but it wasn't because I was leaving Kj. Cori had raised Kj since he was a baby while Kenny and I laid up most of the time. Why the change now?

"Why are you really upset? It can't be because I'm leaving my son. You've never had a problem with that before, so why now?" I asked.

"I like seeing you in your mother role. I'm not sure what this baby is doing to you, but I like it. I liked the way we could co-parent Kj without the arguing," Kenny spoke.

"I'm sorry, but Novi is my husband. You had that chance but didn't take it. I'll make sure to call Kj every night and I'll send money every week too."

"Keep your money, he don't need it."

Kenny snatched up Kj's stuff and headed to the car.

"Kj, come give me a kiss," I called out to him.

"I love you, Paris," Kj said.

"Mommy loves you, too, Kj. I'll let you visit me soon. I'll call you every night, too, okay?"

"Okay."

Kj took off running so his daddy could help him in the car. Once Kenny got him in the car, he took one last look at me before he got in his car and pulled off. The tears fell from my eyes after they pulled off. For once in my life, I was being a mother and it was snatched away in the blink of an eye.

♥

"You look beautiful." Novi kissed my shoulder as we exited the plane.

I might have looked beautiful, but I felt like trash. Since I'd been on this plane with Novi, I thought about my options. If I had stayed home, would he have killed me, or would he have waited until I birthed his child? I was still confused on why he wanted me so bad when he had a whole man at home.

Novi rubbed on my stomach the whole time we rode to his house.

"You don't have to tense up. He's about to leave, trust me," Novi reassured.

"Before I get out, I think I deserve to know if you're in a relationship with a man," I said.

"I'm in a relationship with you." He kissed my lips and got out.

As Novi helped me out the car, I could feel someone's eyes on me. I looked at the front door, and there he stood, with his hands on his hips and a mug on his face.

"Didn't know you were coming back with this whale."

"Moody, don't make me snap your neck. Your flight leaves early in the morning, so go get some rest and stop worrying about my wife," Novi told him.

A smile crept across my face. I even winked at him to piss him off even more. Seeing him stomp off like the diva he was gave me the satisfaction I needed. Novi gave my bags to his staff as he grabbed my hand and walked me out to my favorite place. It was a place that overlooked the backyard. I would always sit out here and think about life. I was almost thirty and life was coming at me fast. I was about to be a mother of two kids and it was time to figure out what I wanted out of life instead of depending on the fathers of my children to finance my expensive lifestyle. Novi put his hand on my knee.

"What are you thinking about, Paris?" Novi asked.

"Nothing," I dryly responded.

"I think we really need to start over and get this thing right. I know I told you we have an agreement, but I don't want to live by that anymore. I want you to be my equal."

Novi pulled the contract out and ripped it up.

"Why did you do that?" I asked.

"Paris, forget the contract. The one you stole was not the original. You're about to have a baby and I don't want us to parent like we're not connected. How can we connect?"

"Novi, I don't want to connect with someone who's not truthful."

"You want the truth, Paris? Is that what your issue is? Okay, now once I tell you this, your only way out is death." He stared at me.

There was something in his voice that reminded me of the day he killed that woman in his office. It was another side of Novi, another life perhaps that he was keeping from me.

"Still want to know?" he asked.

"No."

"Either way, Paris, the only way out is death. I'll be back before dinner is ready." He kissed my lips, followed by my stomach, then left.

I grabbed the glass of tea that was sitting on the table next to me and took a sip. The sun was shining so beautifully. All I could hear was Novi's voice when he said death. I laid my head back and closed my eyes.

"You really think I'm about to let you come in here and mess up what I got going on?" Moody asked.

"Please don't come out here bothering me. I'm only here to have this baby. Whatever y'all got going on has nothing to do with me."

"It has a lot to do with you. You've come in and got yourself pregnant and you think Novi wants you? Ha! You're not his type boo boo. You'll have that baby and he'll kill you and send your body back home. You've got to be the dumbest person he's been with. I know why he went and got an American girl. You're clueless about what's going on here. Just so you know, I don't like you or that baby you're carrying."

I tried to sit up, but he yanked me back down with a cord around my neck. I wasn't a punk, but Moody was still a man with a little more strength than me.

"Listen up and I want you to listen clearly. Novi does not belong to you. When you have that baby, rather, *if* you have this baby, I want you to leave and never come back. If you don't, then you'll be seeing my face again, but the next time you'll be staring death in the face. I would hate to show you that I'm really not one to play with."

He squeezed the cord tighter around my neck until I was struggling to breathe. The more I tried to relieve the pressure on my throat, the tighter he squeezed.

"No need to worry. I didn't plan on killing you today," he said before releasing me.

I sat in the chair, fighting to catch my breath. I literally hated myself for even getting involved with Novi. He was keeping secrets and I had to sleep in the house with a man I didn't know. Novi said he wasn't in a relationship with him, but the way he was acting told me something different. I slipped into my room and locked the door. One thing I didn't play about was someone threatening me or putting their hands on me. I took a quick shower and changed into something a little more comfortable. Since I was back in the house, I planned on investigating what was going on around me.

It was now almost nine, and again, just like before, Novi was not home and I was forced to eat dinner with Moody. I wasn't in the mood to eat what was cooked, so I tried to skip dinner until Novi called and fussed about me not feeding the baby.

"There you are." Moody's voice echoed through the dining room.

"Why do you insist on me eating dinner with you?"

"We're like sister wives, so we might as well get used to it." He smiled.

"I'm not very hungry. I ate something on the flight."

"Paris, shut up and eat before you magically disappear. I'm being nice here, so let's enjoy our dinner together."

I still didn't eat because I didn't trust Moody. I drunk some of my tea and ate the salad that didn't look like it had been tampered with. Moody stared at me as I ate the salad with a small grin on his face. It was then that I put my fork down and excused myself from the table. If I got hungry throughout the night, I would make a sandwich or something. When I made it to my room, I locked the door and climbed into bed.

A slap to my bare face woke me up out of my sleep. Before I could fully open my eyes, I was snatched out of bed and dragged into the bathroom and into a tub full of cold water.

"You know what I don't like, Paris? Females like you. You think because you're pretty, you dress nice and you smell good, all men want you. But see, you're wrong, Paris. Novi doesn't want you. He wants me. I went and got my butt and boobs done thinking that would make him want me, but to my surprise, I come back and here you are," Moody aggressively said.

"But I didn't—" That was all I was able to say before he pushed me under the water. I kicked and even tried to scream, but my mouth filled with ice cold water. I hated that this baby made me sleep so hard. I hadn't heard Moody come into my room at all.

"Breathe, whore." Moody pulled me up from the cold water.

"Please, Moody, you're going to hurt my baby," I begged.

Grabbing my hair, he pushed me back down under the water. I was freezing and my lungs were filling up with water. I tried to hold my breath as long as I could. I opened my eyes to see Moody smiling and blowing kisses at me. I was tired of fighting, so if faking like I had passed out was going to get him to leave me alone, then so be it.

"Paris! Paris, baby, get up… What were y'all doing? I asked y'all to watch her while she was pregnant. Just move…move out the way." I heard Novi fussing.

"Sir, she left dinner upset and we didn't see her anymore. I thought she was resting," one of the ladies said.

Novi's big arms scooped me out of the water. The warmness of his body gave me the strength to open my eyes.

"Give me some towels and the comforter off the bed."

"But she's wet, sir. The comforter cost you thousands."

"Do I look like I give a damn about money right now? My wife is freezing and her lips are blue," he yelled.

"Nov...Novi," I whispered before I started coughing up water.

"Where is Dr. Blanko?"

"I called him, sir. He stated it would take him at least ten minutes to get here."

"It's been ten minutes." Novi continued to fuss.

Water spilled from my mouth every time I tried to say something. I was glad I was getting it out, but something didn't feel right. I was trying to tell him that my stomach was cramping, but the pain that shot up my back sent me into shock.

Novi

"What took you so long?" I asked Dr. Blanko. "Please, lay her here. She doesn't look good," he replied.

I laid Paris in the bed like he asked and paced the floor as he took her vitals. I knew she wasn't doing well by the concerned look on Dr. Blanko's face.

"Novi, she has to get to the hospital. She's freezing and I don't have the right equipment to get her warmed up fast enough. From the sound of her lungs, she still has fluid in them and—"

"And what?" I walked up to him.

"She's bleeding and could possibly lose the baby."

"How fast can you get her to the hospital?"

"You're pretty far away, but I can get a good friend to land his helicopter here and take her. You got to get him a clear space to land, though," Dr. Blanko expressed.

I ran and got my staff to get everything set up for his landing. I could not lose my child, or Paris for that matter. I had plans and this wasn't part of it. I ran in every bedroom and grabbed as many covers as I could to lay on top of Paris. She was unresponsive at the time and I was scared out of my mind.

When I got the text from Moody telling me that Paris hadn't come down for dinner, I didn't think anything of it. I thought she was just being a brat because she didn't like Moody, but he was starting to really look like the brat. Paris loved herself too much to kill herself, so this tub full of ice water had his name all over it.

After making sure Paris was secured in the helicopter, I jumped in my Wraith and headed towards the hospital. Paparazzi was already there, taking pictures but I didn't have time to be pissed off or argue with them. I rushed into the hospital, only to get stopped by the nurse.

"I'm sorry, but you have to wait out here. She's in very bad shape and until we can get her stable and the police come and talk to her, you are not allowed in the back," the nurse said.

"Are you insinuating I did this?" I asked her, getting down to her level so she could see me.

"Again, sir, you have to wait out here."

"If you're not out here in the next hour telling me how my wife and unborn child is doing, I swear you will not like me," I told her.

She turned around with her head up in the air. I didn't care if I had hurt her feelings or not. I would never hurt Paris intentionally. I took a seat and pulled my phone out to call Moody. I knew for a fact his flight didn't leave until ten. It wasn't strange that he wasn't there because he could've been turning tricks, but I did find it strange that he hadn't called and checked in.

"Hello?" Moody answered in a sing-song voice.

"Where are you?"

"I'm working, but of course you knew that already."

"What time did you leave home tonight?"

"I don't know, I think right after dinner."

"Did you see Paris before you left?" I continued to question.

"No, she left dinner upset because she couldn't stand sitting with me. I tell you, that girl is dysfunctional, and if you don't hurry up and do something with her, I'm sure she's going to hurt someone. And this is the person you wanted to have a baby with," Moody finished.

"I don't think Paris is the problem here, I think you are."

"What do you mean?"

"I mean someone left my wife in a tub full of ice cold water. If I hadn't got home in time, I'm sure she would've died. You wouldn't know anything about that, would you?"

"What! Are you saying I tried to hurt her? I wouldn't do anything like that knowing she's pregnant. I know how much this baby means to you. My feelings are hurt, Novi."

"I don't care about your feelings right now. I don't trust anyone, and until I find out who did this, everyone will get treated the same, including you."

"What do you mean by that?"

"You're just a worker, Moody. You will no longer have access to my house. I'll be changing the locks immediately. All staff will have to check in with me when they get there and when they leave. I'll make sure to have some cameras installed in my home as well. This will not happen again. Have a safe trip, Moody," I stated before hanging up.

As I waited for an update on Paris, I started firing some of my staff. It was cruel, but it was something that had to be done. I paid them generously and they couldn't do their job. Some of them were so scared of Moody that when he came around, they were frightened to speak to me. Moody had another side to him that I hadn't seen because I was hardly around.

"Sir, we have your wife stable. The police will be here soon and they may question you as well. After they leave, you'll be able to go back and see her," the nurse stated.

I shook my head at her because she was still trying to say I had done this. I would be a fool to still be sitting here. I watched as the officers walked in and were escorted to Paris' room. They stayed back there for at least thirty minutes before they came back. They took one look at me and kept walking. I got up and went to the nurses' station.

"Can I go see my wife now?"

"She's in the last room on the right." She rolled her eyes at me.

I briskly walked towards her room and when I entered, she was laying there with her hand on her stomach. I felt better knowing she was still pregnant. She didn't even look at me, but I still took the chance to walk up to her and touch her stomach.

"How are you?" I asked.

"I want to go back home. I don't want to be here with your jealous boyfriend. If he did this and he finds out that he didn't kill me?"

"He's not going to hurt you. He's gone. How do you know he did this?" I eyed her.

"Are you kidding? I saw him. We had a conversation. I begged him to stop before he dipped me in the water for the last time. I had to lay under the water and pretend to be dead for him to stop. I thought I would be able to stay under there until he left, but he sat on the edge of the tub, smoking a cigarette and talking on the phone. Everything was muffled so I couldn't hear who he was talking to. I thought it was something y'all planned," she explained.

"You think I would do something like this? I'll handle Moody, but you cannot go back home."

"Novi, if I stay here, I want my own place. I can't go back to that house."

I wrapped my hands around Paris' neck and squeezed lightly. "You will go and do as I say. When you are released from here, you will be coming home with me. If I tell you I'm going to handle something, then let me do that."

Paris gave me the stare of death and I let her go.

"Rest up and I'll see you tomorrow."

"You know I'm losing the baby, right? If I lose it, then there is no more use for me here in Brazil. That is the only reason I'm here, right?" Paris yelled at my back.

"You will not lose the baby. I'll make sure you're on strict bed rest, only getting up to use the bathroom. I know you don't want to keep the baby because you want to go home. If I find out you're behind this, I promise you I'll kill everyone connected to you. For your sake, you better clamp your legs and hold that baby in as long as you can," I said before walking out, bumping into the nurse.

"Is everything okay in there?" She looked over my shoulder.

"Don't worry about my wife and me. We good. Just do your job and make sure she doesn't lose my baby."

Cori

"You look so nervous. Calm down, everything is going to be fine. You look real good, by the way," Syeer stated.

"Thank you. I haven't met someone's parents in years. I hope they don't jump down my throat about what I'm wearing."

"You look good, trust me. My mama is probably dressed just like this. She thinks she's a young tenderoni." Syeer laughed.

We were sitting outside of his parents' house and my nerves were getting the best of me. My guts were bubbling and I needed an anxiety pill or something. Syeer got out and came on my side to open the door for me. He held his hand out to help me get out and I took his hand and stepped out of the vehicle.

"Take a deep breath. I want you to be yourself. Everyone here is going to love you just the way you are."

I inhaled and exhaled as we made our way to the door.

"You took your wedding ring off?" Syeer lifted my hand.

"It's in my purse. I didn't want them questioning me about it," I whispered as the door popped open.

"Syeer, if you don't get in here. I was just telling everyone you were coming. Oh my, who is this gorgeous woman?" a woman who looked similar to Syeer asked.

"Hey, mama," Syeer greeted her with a kiss on her rosy cheeks. "This is my friend and date for tonight, Cori."

"Well, heyyyyy, Cori. Come on and give me a hug." She pulled me in for an embrace.

We walked in the house and the dinner party was already jumping. I saw where Syeer got his class from because his parents' home was gorgeous. He was right about one thing: his mother was dressed in a tight off the shoulder dress. I still hadn't seen his father yet, but I was sure he wasn't far away.

"There's my son," a handsome male interrupted us.

"What's up, dad?" Syeer dapped his father up.

The way he eyed me made me feel naked in front him. He was very handsome, maybe even better than Syeer. I wasn't into older men, though, so it was definitely a turn-off.

"Adrian, why are you staring at the poor girl like that? You're scaring her," Syeer's mother stated. "I'm sorry, my husband is being so rude. This is my husband, Adrian, and you can just call me Kee for short."

"Son, what happened to your other girlfriend?" his father asked.

"Dad, don't do that in front of my company. Cori knows all about my past relationships," Syeer reassured him.

He shook his head and took a glance at me again before his wife pulled him away. There was something weird about him. He was very disrespectful to stare at me like he was with his wife in the same room.

"Please excuse my dad. He's very outspoken."

"It's okay."

Syeer and I mingled with some of his cousins who were our age before we all sat around the table to eat. When his mother called for all of us to gather around the table, I sat next to Syeer and his mother. I felt better because she was blocking Adrian's view. He tried his hardest to get my attention with his eyes, but I wouldn't dare make contact.

"My son tells me you pulled your first big gig this week." Kee broke the silence on our side of the table.

"Yes, I'm very grateful to have your son on my team. He helped make me what I am today," I told her.

"Tell us about you. Who is Cori?" she poked.

"I'm really a nobody. I work, go home and take care of my nephew."

"No kids?" Adrian asked.

"No kids," I replied with a sad look.

"You're still young, they will come." His mother squeezed my hand.

"Maybe." I gave her a faint smile.

The rest of the dinner went off well. I kept checking my watch because I knew Mari would be at my house soon and I wanted to get there before he caught me getting out of the car with Syeer. Mari was spending more time at home than expected. He was slowly moving his stuff back in and his phone was constantly ringing because of his child's mother, but he reassured me I had nothing to worry about.

"Are you ready to go? I see you keep looking at your watch," Syeer whispered.

"No, I'm fine," I lied.

"You know it's cool with me, right? We just kicking it. Ain't nothing serious if you trying to make it back home before hubby gets there," he whispered in my ear.

The touch of his lips on my earlobe sent chills down my back. My heart was racing and I knew it was time to go. I was still married and a man wasn't supposed to make me feel this way. I made a vow and I was going to stick by it.

"We about to head out of here. I got to get Cori home before it gets too late."

"Why you rushing off?" his father asked.

"We've been here for hours, dad. It's kind of late."

"Adrian, let them children go and enjoy the rest of their night," his mother interjected.

Syeer pulled my chair out so I could get up. I thought I heard his father make a noise, but maybe I was hearing things.

"I'll walk y'all out," his mother said.

"Cori, we need to hang out one day. Just us girls. I think we have a lot in common," Kee said once we made it to the car.

"I'll make sure to get with you. It was nice meeting you," I told her.

"You take care of her, son." She kissed him.

We rode in silence all the way to my house. When he pulled up, I was kind of disappointed that Mari wasn't there.

"How long you gon' do this with him, Cori?" Syeer broke the silence.

"Huh?"

"Don't huh me. If you can huh, you can hear. I can tell when your husband is home because your attitude is always chipper at work and I can tell when he stood you up, like now. I like it better when you're happy. You smile more and I get to see the cute little dimple on your left cheek."

"He's my husband. What am I supposed to do? I can't just leave him because he messed up."

"I'm not asking you to leave him because, obviously, you love him. However, you do need to put yourself first for once.

You were excited to get home and leave me to be with him but look, he ain't even here."

"You don't have to rub it in. My feelings are hurt enough, please don't make it worse," I stressed.

"Aye, hold your head up. I'm not about to let you be all down around me about a dude who's confused about what he wants. There is no way you could be my woman right now. I'll be up under you so much you'll beg me to go hang with the fellas."

"Quit trying to blow my head up."

"I'm for real. Cori, you cool to hang around. You look good, you can cook, your house stays clean, but most of all, your heart is so pure. I see how you love everyone else, but it's hard for you to love yourself. I pay attention to you, Cori. I know you don't like your food touching, you don't like anything grape, you like old school R&B, you know, the music way before your time. Your favorite time of the year is fall, you like sunflowers and you like ratchet television shows," Syeer spilled.

"You are a creep." I laughed.

"I'm not a creep, I'm just observant. I watch you, so when it's my time to have you, I know how to treat you."

His comment threw me off. I looked at him to make sure he was talking about me. My own husband didn't know what flower I liked or what my favorite time of the year was. I'd only known Syeer for a few months and he knew everything that made my heart tick or my skin crawl. He was staring at me and I was left without anything to say.

"I better get you in the house, it's getting late."

"Thank you, Syeer."

"You don't have to thank me for anything. I'm doing what your husband should've been doing all those years he had you."

Syeer walked me to the door, but a part of me didn't want him to leave. We stood on my porch for the longest like we were teenagers waiting on each other to take the first step. Syeer placed his hand on my face and caressed my cheek. I couldn't look at him because I knew what I wanted to do was wrong. My body was reacting and I wasn't thinking straight. He lifted my head and placed a soft but passionate kiss on my lips.

"I'll see you Monday, Cori."

"O…okay." I fumbled with my keys.

Hearing Syeer chuckle behind me made me nervous. I was out here acting like a teenage virgin. I finally was able to get the key in the door, but I wanted to know why I had to wait until Monday to see him. I didn't want to come off wrong, so I walked in the house and stood behind the door as Syeer walked backward to his car, licking those gorgeous pink lips he had just kissed me with. I slammed the door and ran to the shower.

Stripping out of my clothes, I placed my body under the cold shower. I needed something to take my mind off him. I showered and tied my braids up in a bun. It was almost eleven at night, but I was about to rearrange my room and clean up the rest of the stuff Mari had brought back home.

♥

It was a Sunday and I woke up feeling refreshed. I went to the bathroom to get myself together before I started placing Mari's stuff in the trunk of my car. I had already texted him and told him I needed to meet him as soon as possible. It was now time for me to wake up and start living for myself. I wasn't about to play number two when I was supposed to be number one in my husband's life. I opted to meet him in a public place in case he wanted to spazz and throw a fit because I was done.

I pulled up to a public park where there were joggers out all times of the day. I smiled as I watched a father push his son on the swings. When I looked a little closer, it was Kj. I jumped out of the car to go see him. Paris' relationship with me was dwindling, but she knew I was always here for her. I blamed it on her pregnancy hormones.

"Hey, y'all. Where is Paris?" I asked, looking around.

"I'm assuming she didn't tell you," Kenny stated. "Kj, go get on the slide while I talk to your auntie."

"What's going on?" I asked, concerned.

"He came and got her and took her back with him. I thought she had changed, Cori, but she picked him over us," Kenny expressed.

I knew he still had feelings for Paris. He didn't think I caught that 'us' but I caught it.

"Something is going on with Paris, and as her friend, I can't really discuss it, but trust me, she is changing. You just have to give her time. You did break her heart pretty bad. Because of that, she's been on a rampage with men. So, are you keeping Kj, or do you want me to take him back? You know I don't mind."

"He's with me now. I missed enough of his life already."

"And the wife?"

"She mad or whatever, but it's cool. We rocky right now anyway. The only thing that matters to me is my son and Paris' well-being."

"You missing her, I see."

"Cori, you know I love Paris' crazy behind. She's like the apple of my eye. I messed up playing with her heart, but I thought I was showing her that I wanted her when I was spending all my time with her and Kj."

"Paris doesn't do well with signs." I laughed. "She's the wild friend; you have to come out and say what you want with her."

"She hasn't called since she left a few days ago and she promised Kj she would FaceTime him every night," Kenny explained.

"When I leave here, I'll try to call her," I told him.

"What you doing here anyway?"

"I'm meeting Mari."

"Oh, I got you. I'm about to take Kj home, keep me updated."

I kissed Kj and tickled him so I could hear that funny laugh before I focused my attention on my husband walking towards me. I gave him his time with Kj while I walked back to my car to pop the trunk.

"What's up?" Mari squeezed my behind and pushed up on me.

"Mari, get off me." I pushed him off.

"What's your problem today?"

"I can't do this back and forth with you, Mari. I just wanted to meet you and bring you your stuff that you were sliding back in the house."

"I don't need you to bring me nothing. I still pay the bills there."

"Because you're supposed to because that's where you're supposed to be, dummy," I argued, as I pulled his stuff out of my trunk.

"You call me all the way here to do this in front of all these people?"

"Boy please, ain't nobody paying us any attention."

"Cori, you really pissing me off. You mad because I didn't come through last night?"

"Listen to you. You saying come through like I'm the side piece. Get your stuff so I can leave." I closed my trunk.

"Cori, I'm not moving anything and you're going to stand here and listen to what I got to say." Mari grabbed me, yanking me towards him.

"I'm not listening to any more lies from you. Leave. Me. The. Hell. Alone," I said through clenched teeth.

Mari grabbed my face and kissed me. I tried to fight, but Mari had a bad effect on me. At this moment, I needed to be strong.

"Cori, I love you so much. Please don't tear up what we have. I'll never love another woman like I love you. Terreka don't mean nothing to me. I'm there for my daughter, and that's it. I haven't slept with her because I've been sleeping with you. Don't do this to us."

"Mari, you did this, not me. No one is getting hurt here but me. Does this Terreka chick know you not feeling her like that?" I asked, staring into his sexy hazel eyes.

"She got to know because I don't even kick it with her like that."

"I got to know what?" a voice said behind us.

I was way shorter than Mari, so I had to peep around him to see who was talking. The woman was pretty, but a little overweight. The scowl on her face reminded me of what Mari and I had just been talking about and the lightbulb went off; this was Terreka.

"You got something you want to tell me, Mari?"

"Terreka, why are you out here? Did you follow me?" Mari asked.

"You left me home with your sick daughter to come out here with her?" She pointed towards me.

"My wife trumps all that bull you spitting. Majesty is fine, she's just teething. If you can't handle that, then you shouldn't be a mother."

"What, just like your wife? She'll never be what I am to you. I don't know what it is about her that keeps you sneaking around."

"I'm standing here, and if you want to address me, then say so. I don't know why you so pissed. I should be the one stomping a mud hole in you right now," I told her.

"Chill out," Mari whispered in my ear.

"You better get your baby mama then."

"Something you'll never be, hunty."

"You got that, but I got papers on him, so you and your baby won't have nothing if something happens to him, just remember that."

"Cori! Did I not just say chill!" Mari yelled.

"This is what I can't deal with. Move off me so I can go. I refuse to sit here and argue with a heifer who don't have sense enough to wash her face before she confronts me," I sassed.

I got into my car and smashed out, leaving them there to argue. Effective tomorrow, I was filing for divorce.

Mari

"While you out here showing your behind, where is Majesty?"

"She's in the car."

"Go home, Terreka," I demanded.

"I'm not leaving until you tell me you coming home behind me." She crossed her arms.

"I'm not coming to your house right now."

"Oh, it's my house now? Say what you trying to say, Mari."

"I'm not saying nothing. I'm trying to leave, but you making a scene about nothing."

"About nothing!" Terreka pushed me.

"Keep your hands to yourself."

"I caught you hugged up with your wife and that's nothing, Mari?"

"Do you hear what you saying right now?" I laughed. "Wife is the keyword in this conversation. I'm free to be with her whenever I want to."

"That's not what you said a few weeks ago. You said you were done with her because you caught her with another dude.

Oh, and you said you were divorcing her so you could marry me. What happened to that?"

"I lied, Terreka, okay? I'll never leave my wife for you. What me and you have is different. You gave me something she couldn't give me, but that doesn't change my love for her. Yea she was old fashion and acted like a prune at one point in our marriage, but I know you saw how fine she is. I caught you taking her in. I hate to hurt your feelings, but you can't hold a candle to my wife, Terreka."

Seeing the tears streaming down her face made me feel bad. She always put me in a situation where I had to pick consoling her or chasing my wife. For now, I was going to console her because we were in front of a crowd.

"Come on. I'll follow you home," I told Terreka.

As I followed Terreka, I thought about Cori. I called her, but she ignored my calls until she finally turned the phone off. Once I got Terreka settled, I was leaving and heading to my house. I had left all my clothes at the park. I was sure someone could use them more than me. We finally made it back to her house and she wasn't as upset as she had been at the park a few minutes ago. She was actually smiling as she kissed on Majesty. I know in her mind she thought she had won, and maybe she had at this point. This was my biggest regret so far: getting her pregnant.

172

I blew out hot air as I got out of the car. Why did I feel like Majesty was a crutch for me? The only reason for me being here was her. If it were up to me, Majesty would be Cori's and I could have my wife back. When we made it in the house, I knew Terreka was about to be on some bull. When she placed Majesty in her bassinet that sat in the living room and placed her hands on her wide hips, it was an obvious sign.

"Why were you at the park with her?" Terreka asked.

"Are we going to argue about something I already told you, or are we going to take care of Majesty since she's so sick?" I inquired.

"Mari, you owe me an explanation for your actions. What you telling me is not what you're showing me right now."

"Terreka, you really need to get it through your head that I don't owe you anything. I owe her. I'm going to tell you this. I should've never left her to be with you but I'm here now and I'm going to make the best of the situation," I explained.

"Well leave, Mari. I'm not going to beg you to stay here with us. I'm tired of you putting her before us anyway."

That's all I needed her to say. I grabbed my keys and headed for the door.

"Mari, we're both upset. Please don't leave me like this. We can just leave it alone and I promise not to bring it up anymore," Terreka cried.

I hated for women to cry. It always tugged at my heart.

"I'll be back," I said over my shoulder.

"You're going to check on her now, right?"

"Yea," I said as I closed the door.

I made the drive over, but Cori's car wasn't there. I tried to call Paris, but she didn't answer. I waited on her for over two hours before I sent her a text. She responded, but it wasn't what I wanted to hear. She had pretty much told me she wasn't coming home. I got out to see if she had left a window or something unlocked.

"Umm, do I need to call the cops?" my neighbor asked.

"What you calling them for? You know this my house as long as you stayed next to us. Your son even played with my nephew. Mind your business."

"I'm just saying, she has another man over here late at night, so I thought she had moved on." She laughed before walking off. "He fine too."

Hearing that irritated me. I knew it was her co-worker, but why was he in my house? I pulled my phone out and called Cori.

"Aye, I don't care what you got to do, but you need to get here right now," I barked into the phone.

"Mari, get off my phone. I'm tired and you are the last person I want to talk to."

"Okay, no problem. You gon' regret not coming home." I hung up the phone in her face.

In a jealous rage, I picked up a loose brick from our landscape and threw it through the window so I could reach in and unlock the door. I shut the alarm off and cleaned the glass up. It was late in the evening and I had a homeboy who fixed broken windows. I called him up and went and took a shower. I fixed some leftovers and waited for Cori to come home. The window was now fixed and it was now almost midnight when her headlights shone through the open window. I was furious at this point and I had to talk myself out of not taking my anger out on her.

The look on Cori's face when she opened the door held guilt. Guilt about what was what I was about to find out. I rushed her, pushing her back up against the door.

"Why, as a married woman, you just now coming in the house?" I snapped.

"Mari, please get out of my face. I don't feel good and I'm tired of seeing you for one day."

"So, you went to see your other dude, though, right?" I tightened my arms around her neck.

"Where I've been is not your concern any longer. Hopefully, by tomorrow, I can go file for divorce and we can end this whole thing."

"What did you just say?"

"I want a divorce, Mari."

"That's not about to happen. You can take your little behind up there all you want to, but nothing is going to come out of it."

"You've obviously moved on, so please let me do the same," she choked.

"You really think I'm about to let you go to be with him?"

"Who said anything about being with someone else, Mari? I've given you some of the best years of my life, and finally, finally I feel like I can move on after a few months without you. I thought this was just a little phase and you would come back, but you're not coming back. You only want to lay up with me and slide back in the bed with her. I'm done with it. Period."

"Dammit, Cori." I hit the door, causing her to flinch. "You just don't get it, do you? I'm trying to come home to you, but my daughter needs me."

"You wouldn't have a daughter if you didn't cheat, Mari. Get out of my face," she said, lightly pushing me out the way.

Fighting with Cori was draining me dry. There was no way I was giving up just like that.

"You had that man in my house, Cori?" I finally addressed my real issue.

"Say what?" She stopped in her tracks.

"I'm not repeating myself."

"He has been here. We work closely together, that's it."

"He can't come back here. I've never disrespected you by bringing a woman here."

"Please! Don't come to me about no disrespect. You can leave because I have to work tomorrow, and so do you."

I sat down on the sofa and kicked my shoes off. I wasn't going anywhere tonight, so she might as well take her short behind in the room and I would chill out here. No man was about to come up in my spot and claim what belonged to me. Cori looked at me with an attitude before she went to the room and slammed the door. I didn't plan on bothering her tonight. Pulling covers out of the closet and getting comfy, I turned the television on and drifted off to sleep.

The sound of my phone ringing disturbed my sleep. The television was still on and Cori had thrown some pillows on the sofa. I hit the green button on my phone.

"Yea," I groggily spoke.

"Do you plan on coming home before the sun comes up?" Terreka yelled.

"I am home, but I'll be there before work."

"Mari, Majesty needs you."

"Terreka, stop playing. Every time I don't move when you want me to, you use my daughter."

"I'm serious. I'm getting her dressed for the ER as we speak." Terreka started crying.

"A'ight, I'm on the way to take y'all."

Rubbing the sleep out of my eyes, I got up to go check on Cori before I left. I wasn't about to leave without telling her. When I opened the door, she wasn't in bed. Following the sound to the bathroom, I hoped I didn't catch her on the phone with this dude. I pushed the bathroom door open to Cori throwing up in the toilet.

"You okay, bae?"

"I'm good. I ate something that didn't settle on my stomach," she replied, wiping her mouth.

Looking at her suspiciously, my mind told me it was deeper than what she was telling me.

"You want me to run you a bath?"

"No, I'm good."

"I got to run and take Majesty to the ER. Can I take you out after work tomorrow so we can talk?"

She nodded her head, confirming our date. I kissed her forehead and helped her back to bed before I left. Cori was pregnant and didn't want to tell me. We had been down this road several times already, so there was no need of getting my hopes up.

Paris

I was now seven months pregnant and Novi hadn't been home for about a month now. He made sure I didn't leave the house or do anything. I would spot here and there, so I was put on strict bed rest. Novi had hired people to bathe me, shop for me, feed me and watch me go to the bathroom. It was disgusting to me. I was actually ready to have this baby so I could have my body and life back. It was now noon and the nurse he had hired was about to come in with something for me to eat or drink. Because I couldn't get out of bed much, I had gained over seventy pounds.

"Paris, I have your lunch," the young Brazilian chick said.

"I'm not hungry."

"Oh, but you must eat. Mr. Novi will kill me."

"Well, you eat it. I just ate three hours ago," I yelled, startling her.

She placed the plate down and headed for the door.

"Look, I'm sorry. I didn't mean to yell at you I'm just tired of this. How much is he paying you?" I asked her.

"Paying? I'm not getting paid. My pay is him keeping me off the streets."

"I'm confused. You are a nurse, right?"

"Yes, but a pretty girl like me gets thrown into the prostitution ring."

I was oblivious to what was going on in the streets of Brazil since Novi never really let me explore like I wanted to.

"Wait, what do you mean?"

"I'm a prostitute. Yes, I'm a nurse, but I was propositioned to make more money by having sex with tourist and other men around the world. When I found out Mr. Novi had another position available, I asked if I could have it. I was tired of living that lifestyle. I originally came here from Barbados to visit and I ended up staying. It's a different world out there, Ms. Paris."

I was taking in everything she was saying. I caught that she went to Novi for another position. Was Novi running this prostitution ring? All the money he flashed and spent reminded me that it wasn't coming from basketball. His season was over, but the money was still coming in.

"You said you went to my husband for a new position?"

"Yes, I was like one of his main girls. He was upset at first, but he said your health was more important and he knew my nursing skills were superb."

"All this time you've taken care of me, I've never asked your name," I told her.

"Aajah."

"Aajah, thank you, and I will make sure to eat the lunch. Can you give me about fifteen minutes alone?" I asked her.

"Yes, sure."

She walked out the room, leaving me to think about everything she had just told me. I took the lunch she brought and placed it in the trash can, then eased into the bathroom to take a quick shower. She would be back in fifteen minutes and I wanted to be dressed and back in bed. There was nothing worse than another woman washing you between your legs when you were fully capable of doing it yourself. It made us both uncomfortable. I planned on using Aajah to my advantage. She freely gave information and my ghetto side loved it.

"Did you want more food, Ms. Paris?"

"Oh, no. I'm full, and please stop calling me Ms. I'm sure we are the same age."

"I apologize. Mr. Novi told everyone to address you as such."

"What else did my husband tell you to do?"

Just like I wanted, she sat down and contemplated whether she should talk or not. I gave her my best smile as she took in a deep breath before she spoke.

"I don't know much, but being his main money maker, I was privy to certain information. I know he was starting to fall for you and he was upset when Moody hurt you. Moody has been trying to get with Novi for years. Novi won't give him the time of day, though. Between the two of us, Novi was able to rake in millions in untaxed money. Moody tried to take me out a few times, but he didn't stand a chance against a west indies girl like myself. I heard Novi telling his body guard, which is his best friend, that he had to stay away from you because y'all's relationship was supposed to be business, but you were starting to pull at his heart. I know about him threatening to kill you if necessary, but it was only to scare you. I think."

"You obviously know way more than me. Have you slept with my husband?"

"Only once. It was before he married you, though. I have no feelings for him. Novi is very ruthless once he deems you useless," she finished.

"Well, I appreciate you telling me how much Novi supposedly loves me, but I ain't believing it. You've been here for some time now and you know he hasn't been home. I'm a girl from the streets. I'm very straightforward and I like my men the same way. Novi can kiss where the sun don't shine unless I'm sitting on Miami Beach."

"Are you ready for your bath now?"

"No, I've already taken my bath and I won't need you bathing me any longer. I can do it alone. You don't have to tell Novi because it ain't that deep."

"Is there anything else you need from me?"

"No, I'm good."

She left out the room, closing the door behind her. I got out of bed and grabbed my phone to call Cori back. I talked to her a few times a week but hadn't built up the nerve to talk to my son. I believed it was because I would have to hear Kenny's voice. I had started to miss both of them.

"Cori," I whispered in the phone.

"Why are you whispering?"

"I need a favor."

"What kind of favor can I do for you and you're thousands of miles away?" Cori asked.

I swear if she weren't my best friend, she wouldn't have any friends. I rolled my eyes at her dumb question.

"I need you to call Novi and tell him you need me to come home because something has happened to my son."

"How am I supposed to call that man?"

"Is this coming from the same person who was responsible for that dumb behind class reunion? How did you get in touch with him then?"

"Social media, dummy. You're his wife; why don't you just give me his number?"

Cori had me on that. I didn't have Novi's new number. He had changed it so much and had never given it to me. Everyone in the house had it but me. I had to come up with a quick lie because Cori picked up on stuff quickly.

"You don't have his number, do you?"

"I do have his number, I just didn't want to give it to you."

"What I want with it? I got enough problems going on with me; I definitely don't want your man," she replied with an attitude.

"You okay, Cori?"

"Yea, it's just Mari and his indecisiveness. It's stressing me out. I'm worried about you. I don't know if I'm coming or going these days."

"Don't worry about me. I'll be home as soon as I have this baby. Unless you call Novi, of course," I reminded her.

"I tell you what. I need to get away, so why don't I come to you? I got some vacation time to use."

"Umm, no, don't do that."

"Why not? I always wanted to go to Brazil, and now that I have the money, it's a perfect time."

I thought about what she said. Novi couldn't be mean if Cori were here. Maybe with her here, I could get a little freedom to at least leave the room.

"Okay, just let me know when you're coming."

"I'll put the time in when I go to work tomorrow and I'll let you know. Paris, you really need to call Kenny and Kj. They…I mean, Kj misses you."

"I don't want to hear Kenny's mouth. He gets a little too flip and I can't stand it. And if his wife answers the phone, we gon' really have a problem," I told her.

"Just call, Paris. You never know what's going on. You always jump on the pole with the most money, not realizing that waiting sometimes pays off. I'll talk to you when I book my flight."

Cori

"Are you sure this is what you want to do?" Syeer asked me.

I held the divorce papers in my hand with tears in my eyes. It had been two weeks since I had sat down and talked with Mari. He had made a promise to move back in, and he did for two days until I came home from work and he was gone, leaving only a note behind. I was leaving to go be with Paris for a week and I wanted to give it to him and leave so he would have time to calm down.

"I think I'm doing the right thing. We're just playing tag team with him. She has him because she gave him something I can't. I cannot compete with that man's baby."

Syeer just listened. He didn't give any suggestions. He never did, and I liked him for that. He didn't judge Mari either, which showed how mature he was. Most men would be trying to make the other man look bad so they could slide in, but Syeer didn't do that.

"I'm here if you need me, but you know that already. I'm about to head to the gym. I'll be back to take you to the airport." Syeer kissed my forehead.

I walked him to the door, and when I opened it, there stood Mari with a mug on his face. Even with the mug, he was still sexy. I looked from Mari to Syeer. I was way too small to even try to stand in between these two giants. Syeer had Mari in the weight and height department, but Mari was far from a pushover.

"Didn't I tell you not to have him in my house?" Mari asked through gritted teeth.

"No need to get all hostile with the lady. I was just leaving," Syeer said nicely.

"I ain't even talking to you. I'm talking to my wife. And since you was leaving, leave!"

Syeer threw his hands up and walked out laughing.

"I'll be back, Cori," he added before walking towards his car.

"Look here, bruh, don't come back to my house I pay bills in. Come back, and see what I do," Mari spat.

"You a real funny cat. Like I just told her, I'll be back. Unlike you, I know she's leaving for a week, so as a man, it's my responsibility to help her carry her luggage and make sure she has everything she needs. But you wouldn't know much about being a man, would you?"

Mari charged at Syeer, but Syeer pulled his gun and placed it on Mari's forehead before he could let off the first punch.

"I've been nice, bruh, but I'm really, really not the man you want to play with. I'm licensed to carry and I feel a little threatened, you feel me? Now, go in your little house and tend to your wife before your life ends right here in your driveway," Syeer threatened.

"Mari, come in the house, please," I begged him.

"Go on, Mari," Syeer mocked.

I didn't know Syeer had this side to him. I knew he carried a gun, but seeing him handle it the way he did... there was so much I didn't know about him. I pulled on Mari's arm, but he didn't budge. He stood there, staring Syeer in his eyes.

"Mari, please."

"Let my arm go." He pushed me off him and marched into the house.

I gave Syeer a sorrowful look.

"Go see about the crybaby. I'll be back," he said before getting in his car.

I walked into the house and closed the door.

"What the hell is this?" Mari asked, slapping me in the face with the stack of papers.

"I...I was going to talk to you about it, but you haven't been answering my calls," I explained as I picked the papers up.

"Cori, I swear you've got to be the dumbest female on earth. Do you not listen, or do you just do what you want to do?

I bluntly told you we are not getting a divorce. You wasted your money trying to get that started because I'm not signing anything."

"Did you just call me dumb? I am dumb, though. You're right. Why are you here now? You want sex?"

"Nah. I came to spend some time with you."

"Not after two weeks. Let me go get this letter so I can remind you what you said."

"You ain't got to do all that."

"You said you were going to work it out with Terreka and you were sorry for dragging me along, so I figured I would rid myself of you and let her have you fully. You are stressing me the hell out. Do you know your baby mama calls my phone at least seven to ten times a day? Surely, she doesn't have a job because if she did, she wouldn't have time to play on my phone."

"I ain't got nothing to do with all that."

"You're innocent in all of this." I laughed. "You don't have to sign them, just know me and you are over and I'm going to move on with my life. I'm moving out of this house so you won't feel like I can't have company because you pay the bills. I'm capable of doing that myself. I make way more money than you, if I may add."

"Don't throw that up in my face."

"Is there anything else you need?" I waited for him to answer.

The sound of glass clashing caught both of our attention. I started walking towards the living room, but he stopped me.

"Stay here." He pushed me back.

"Mari, get out here!"

"Is that your baby mama in front of my house?" I asked, walking behind him.

"Terreka, don't bust another one of my windows," Mari fussed.

I stood in the doorway, wishing she would continue to tear his car up.

"Why you keep playing me for her?" She waved her bat towards me.

"You better get your girl away from my house before I have both of y'all arrested," I told him.

"Try it, trick. You think you're special, don't you? You ain't nothing but a piece of trash who can't carry a baby," she spazzed.

"I got to be special baby because you're number one now and you still can't keep him. He still keeps running back to me," I mocked her.

She tried to run towards me, but Mari stopped her, throwing her over his shoulder and walking towards her car.

The last time I saw her, she wasn't driving a Benz, she was driving a beat-up Toyota. I knew Mari couldn't afford that, but I didn't care. I shut the door when he threw her in the car and jumped in the driver seat, pulling off.

I leaned on the door because the room was spinning and I didn't feel too well. I already knew what the problem was; I was pregnant, but I hadn't told anyone. I was so used to miscarrying that I didn't want anyone to know. If Mari knew I was keeping this secret from him, he would kill me. I didn't want to tell him because I didn't want him to feel like he would have to choose. I could take care of my child without him.

I made it to the sofa and laid down. My flight left in three hours and I still hadn't finished packing yet. Taking this flight so early in this pregnancy was a risk for me. In my mind, if I was going to be pregnant, then so be it. If I was going to lose it, so be it. My heart was numb to it now. I knew what my chances were when I kept sleeping with Mari whenever he wanted it, knowing he wasn't going to be with me. I squeezed my eyes shut because the room was still spinning. I started to sweat, so I took my shirt off so I could cool off.

I let an hour pass before I was able to get up and start packing. I still didn't feel my best, but I was so excited to hang out with Paris. She had a few more weeks before the baby came and I was ready to buy some gifts. Syeer called, letting me know he was at the door.

"You did that to his car?" Syeer laughed.

"No, his baby mama came and wreaked havoc. He had to carry her away kicking and screaming." I laughed.

"You about ready?"

"No, I got a little sick, so I had to lay down, but I'll be ready in a minute."

"You don't look good. Are you sure you want to take that long flight?"

"I'll be fine."

"I'm worried about you, Cori. You got a lot going on. Postpone the flight for a day or two until you feel better, at least. I can't have you sick or have something happen to you before I get to see how those lips really taste."

My face turned red as he caressed my cheeks.

"I'll pay for your next flight and even give you spending money. Just rest and I'll handle those extra two days at work."

"I swear you be doing the most."

"I got to, baby. I do the most to make sure you're happy."

"I really appreciate you."

"I'm just chilling; this is who I am. Now, when I said rest, I don't mean here. You do know he's going to come back and get his car, right? Just get you some clothes. I'm going to take you to my spot. And no, I'm not going to bother you, unless you want me to." He smiled.

"Don't play."

"I'm not playing. Grown men don't play games, baby. Before I leave this realm, you will be my wife. Now, come on before he comes back and I have to put a bullet between his eyes."

"About that," I started.

"I know it scared you."

"It's just a side of you I hadn't seen."

"There are a lot of sides to me you haven't seen. I only reveal what's needed at the time. I've been burned by love before too. I'll let you peel me back layer by layer. I haven't always been nice. It's like poking a sleeping bear. When he wakes up, everyone is in danger. I'm sorry for scaring you."

I packed a quick overnight bag and we were out the door, headed to his house. I'd known him a few months now and I hadn't been to his place because I didn't think that was the wise thing to do. I always invited him to my place because I felt safe there, or we would meet in a public place to have a drink or two. I fell asleep before we made it to his place. The door popped open on my side and Syeer unfastened my seatbelt and scooped me up into his arms.

"Wait, I need to get my bag so I can bathe."

"I got it. You sleep so hard. I tried to wake you up, but you were out like a light."

"You can put me down. I feel like a toddler in your big arms."

"You not used to this type of treatment I see. I'll put you down, though, because you asked me to," Syeer stated.

He opened the door to his house and was a gentleman by letting me walk in first. It was a typical man's crib, but it was very clean. It was a bit big for a man like Syeer. It had at least four bedrooms. There was no sign of a woman being here at all. Everything was so manly.

"Why do you live in this big house by yourself?"

"I make a lot of money and I always wanted a family, but it never happened. I bought the house anyway, hoping the universe aligned me with someone to have a bunch of kids for me."

I swallowed hard. I definitely wasn't the woman for him. If I would've had all the babies I'd been pregnant with, I would be like the mother in the shoe.

"You don't look like the type to want a lot of kids."

"Stop going by what I look like. I would be a wonderful father. Let me show you where you'll be sleeping."

Syeer carried my bag and purse to the bedroom next to his. It was a nice room, but still manly. The room was navy blue with red accents. I was satisfied that I had my own bathroom, though. Syeer kissed my cheek and told me he would order some food. I ran a hot bath and relaxed. This was the most relaxed I'd been in a while. The jets from the tub eased my tense muscles to the point I drifted off to sleep.

"Girl, I've been calling you for the last ten minutes," Syeer's voice boomed.

I woke up, covering myself, splashing water all over the floor. When I looked up at Syeer, his back was turned to me, so he wasn't even looking. I smiled because he was showing himself to be the perfect gentleman.

"I'm sorry. I don't even remember going to sleep."

"I'm sure the water is cold by now. Put something on and come and join me for dinner." Syeer blindly handed me a towel.

When Syeer walked out, I got out the tub, wrapping the towel around my body. I was cold from the water, but Syeer had adjusted the air in the room and cut the ceiling fan off. It was these things that helped me make my decision to fully leave Mari and try my chances with Syeer. I hadn't told Syeer yet because I didn't know what I wanted to do with this baby. I hadn't set up a doctor's appointment or anything. I didn't want to get attached and then lose it. I threw on some clothes and joined Syeer.

"I don't think I've ever seen you look so comfortable," Syeer said.

"You just going to eat without me?"

"You were taking way too much time just to throw on some jogging pants, bra and t-shirt."

"Whatever. What did you get me?"

Taking the brown bag and opening it, the smell of garlic hit my nose and vomit spilled from my mouth. Syeer rushed to help me, but I was now doubled over, releasing everything from my insides. After I was done, Syeer managed to clean me up and get me in the bed. I was so weak and I felt bad that I couldn't clean up after myself.

"I got everything cleaned. You might want to get to the doctor about that little situation." Syeer gave me some ginger ale.

"I'll be fine."

"Cori, I understand you may be scared, but you've got to go take care of yourself. And that Brazil trip is dead. I'll call Paris myself and tell her. You got a life growing inside of you and flying across the country, ignoring it, ain't the adult thing to do. Does Mari know?" Syeer sat on the edge of the bed.

"I don't want to tell him until I get past a certain trimester. How do you know?" I asked him.

"Cori, you are not the only woman I've been with. Get some rest and I'll see you in the morning. You need to tell him and let him decide if he gon' be with you or not. If not, I'm here. Goodnight, beautiful." He blew me a kiss and closed the door.

Paris

I didn't know why I was so irritated today. Novi was home and I could clearly hear him having sexual relations with another woman in the next room. I didn't have an ounce of feelings for him so I couldn't care less who he was sleeping with. All I wanted was those blue hundreds in my account. The noise finally stopped and I was able to roll out of bed and peep out the door to see who would come out the room first.

"Close the door, Paris." Novi's voice boomed from the room next door.

Today, I felt a little bold. Maybe it was because I had talked to my son a few days ago and I missed him. I was pissed that I had even decided to do this with Novi. He was inconsiderate of my feelings. I was ready to die just to get out of this situation. I went next door and jiggled the door, but it was locked.

"Open the door, Novi!" I yelled, beating and kicking on the door.

"Paris, if you don't get away from that door, I promise you won't like me if I get up."

I continued to show out because I wanted him to open the door enough for me to see who was brave enough to sleep with my husband while I laid right in the other room. The door popped open, almost knocking me over. Novi tried to block me, but my anger took over. Pushing him with all the strength I had, he fell backward and I barged into the room and there laid Aajah. She was covered up with only her eyes peeping out of the cover.

"You lying, dirty hoe." I jumped on the bed and started beating her face with my fist.

I was from the streets, the gutter, the projects or whatever you called your bad neighborhood. Fighting was in my blood. Everyone thought because I was cute, I couldn't throw them hands. It was only when you tried me, I showed you what my mama and all my cousins had taught me.

She scratched me across my face, only adding to her butt whooping. This heifer had been using me the whole time. I thought about how many times she had washed me up and how she had lied and told me she had only slept with him once. A fist connected with the side of my face and the stars I saw slowed me up a bit. It couldn't have been from Aajah, and the only other person in the room was Novi. Another blow came, but this time, I was out cold.

♥

The sound of whispering woke me up. When I tried to sit up, a pain in my stomach caused me to yell out.

"Oh no! Please lay down. You just had major surgery and we don't want you to burst any of your staples," a Brazilian woman stated.

"Where am I?"

"You're at the hospital, and you just gave birth to a beautiful little girl." She smiled.

Rubbing my stomach to confirm what she had just said, it wasn't flat, but it was flatter than it had been. Looking around the room, I didn't see Novi or my daughter.

"She's in the nursery. She was a pretty big baby, weighing almost eight pounds."

How was she so big when I had just turned eight months? Then it hit me. Was this baby Kenny's? I did sleep with him the night before I left to come to Brazil. I pushed that thought out of my mind because surely, the doctors would've known I was already pregnant. Then another light bulb went off. I didn't go to the doctor; Novi always sent someone to the house to see about me.

"Your blood pressure is very high. I'm going to give you something for pain and to get the pressure down. Just relax for tonight and we will let you see your baby tomorrow. We are concerned about you because of the big bruise on your face, but we see so many women like you come in, we don't even bother to ask questions anymore."

When she closed the door, fear came over me because all I could remember was getting into a fight with Aajah and Novi hitting me. I wasn't sure how I had gotten here. Pulling the cover back, I looked at my scar running from my navel to the top of my vagina. The wound was very fresh and even had some blood on it. I really wanted to see my daughter, but the pain medicine was starting to take effect on my body. I tried to keep my eyes open, but it didn't work. Sleep was overshadowing me. I let my heavy eyes close.

"Wake up, sleepyhead."

The sound of Novi's voice made me flinch. I continued to lay there like I was asleep so he would leave. He pulled the cover back and surveyed my body and made grunts as he looked at my stomach. I laid there, hoping he wouldn't want me because of the ugly scar.

"I know you're laying here pretending to be sleep, but as long as you can hear me, that's all I need. When the sun comes up, you will not be laying in this hospital bed. You have served your purpose and given birth to my daughter. Now that you are no longer pregnant, you gotta work. I've tested you and you're clean and ready to make some money. I have someone watching you, so there's no need to run. The men are going to have a field day with you. I can smell the cash coming from your vagina. Rest up, wife," he finished as he placed a kiss on my lips.

The tears spilled down my face when I heard the door close. Novi was a monster and I had bit off more than I could chew. I let the dollar bill control me and now there was no telling what was about to become of my life. I got up to reach for my phone so I could call and talk to Kj or Cori, but it was no longer there. My purse and everything was now gone. I hit the nurses' button to call someone in here to help me.

"Do you need something?" the nurse from earlier asked.

"Is there any way you could let me use a phone or something?"

"Is it a long-distance call?"

"Yes."

"I'm sorry, but the hospital won't allow it. It's too expensive."

"I'm not worried about money. I'll pay the bill."

"I'm sorry, I can't. Is there anything else I can help you with?"

"No, thank you."

This was it. I was stuck, and all my gold digging days had caught up with me. I had nowhere to run or hide that Novi wouldn't find me and kill me. I laid back in bed and cried and waited for him to come back.

Terreka

I waited a whole hour for Mari to go to sleep. I had slipped him some Xanax and melatonin in his food. I needed him to be completely unaware. He was so far up Cori's behind that he hadn't noticed I was sleeping with another man right in our house. Adrian and I had started sleeping together again. We had both agreed that we were young and careless and that was why we had gotten caught by his wife. Mari had asked how I had gotten a new Benz, but I told him I had traded my old car and got this one with little to no money down and he believed me, only because he was on his phone, texting Cori when he asked.

I leaned over to make sure Mari was still breathing before I slipped out of the bedroom. I passed my daughter's room and went into the kitchen to grab my keys. The only thing I needed was my keys and cell phone. I would be back before either of them woke up. I had one destination in mind as I bit down on my bottom lip. The neighborhood was dark, so I shut my lights off and parked at the neighbor's house. She wasn't a big fan of Cori and she had told me out of her own mouth. She was the reason I knew where she lived and when Mari was coming and going.

You could say we had become really good friends. I loved a messy female who liked getting her hands dirty.

Looking up, I could see her standing in her doorway, waving me into the house. I slid out the car and into her house. I only planned on scaring Cori a bit and revealing to her that I was pregnant again so she could leave Mari alone.

"She just got back a few days ago. She been with some dude, chile. I tried to get him to take the bait with his fine self, but he chumped me off so bad I almost cried," she said.

"What side did you say her room was on?" I asked.

"It's the last window on the far back of the house. There's a rose bush right in front of her window."

"Did you get what I needed?"

"I have your gloves here, the hammer is here, and the crowbar is by the front door."

"Thank you," I said as I put the gloves on.

"Oh, and here's the key. It wasn't easy getting this, but Cori is clumsy. The day after Mari left her, she dropped something in the grass while in a rush. I didn't know what it was at the time, but I tried it and it worked to the front door. I'm sure it's Mari's old key."

"Girl, I'm going to end up making you my right hand. I don't need the crowbar now," I told her.

She waited until I was out of her door and in Cori's yard before she shut off all the lights to her house. My heart raced as I put the key in the door. The house was cold and quiet. The glow of light was coming from the light over the stove. It gave me what I needed to move around the house. I opened her refrigerator and emptied out stuff on the floor. I unplugged her deep freezer so all her food would go bad. I went to her living room and pulled out my razor to cut up her furniture. Once I was satisfied there, I moved to the dining room, but there wasn't much to do in there. Some paperwork sat on the table and I opened it out of curiosity and it was a divorce decree filed by Cori. I put it back down and picked up another set of papers from a doctor's office. Covering my mouth, I read the letter over and over. Cori was pregnant. I had to keep Mari from finding out.

I walked until I found her bedroom. Cori laid across the bed, fully clothed like she wasn't supposed to be here but got tired and gave up. She had a suitcase with clothes in it and her cell phone was lit up with text messages. She had to be knocked out because she had text messages from Mari from two hours ago. She had a few from somebody named Syeer and then there was an unknown caller who had called about an hour ago. There were a lot of things I wanted to do to her, but right now, I just wanted to let her know I could get to her. I pulled my pregnancy test out of my pocket and set it right by her nose. I wanted it to be the first thing she saw when she got up. One thing I knew about pretty girls, they didn't have a clue about fighting, so what was she going to do when she found out I had been here? Nothing! I grabbed a chunk of her braids and sliced them off with one swipe, spreading them throughout the house as I left.

I ran to my car, grabbed my spray paint and went back to her car. I left her a little message before I jumped in my car and drove off.

"Welcome to my world, Cori. You want to take what belongs to me? We'll see who's standing at the end." I laughed as I headed home to be with my family.

The finale is coming in September 2017...

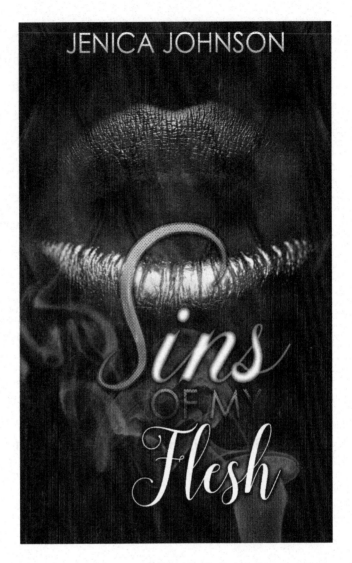

Grab this gut wrenching release while you wait for part 2!

CPSIA information can be obtained
at www.ICGtesting.com
Printed in the USA
LVOW13s2034290118
564435LV00013B/1391/P